BARE ESSENTIALS

The LBD Project, Book 3

Kim Black

Copyright © 2019 Steepledog Productions
ISBN: 978-1-946846-10-5

Published by Steepledog Productions

PO Box 50814

Amarillo, TX 79159

www.kimblackink.com

Printed in the United States of America

Cover design by Samuel and Sean Black

DEDICATION
For my daddy

ACKNOWLEDGMENTS

A special thank you to James D. Quiggle for your killer editing skills. Thank you to Sam and Sean Black for the incredible cover art.

Thank you to my dear Lone Star Women of Letters sister-writers, Donna, Suzana, and Brandi. Thank you for your love and support.

To Riley, thank you for being my partner in this amazing adventure.

ABOUT THE AUTHOR

Kim Black is an award-winning author and designer. She is a member and has served as President of the Texas High Plains Writers, one of the oldest writing organizations in the country.

She has also published historical Christian fiction and children's books under the name Kimberly Black.

She lives in the Texas Panhandle with her husband and grown children.

For more about Kim and her writing, visit her website www.kimblackink.com

MORE BOOKS BY KIM BLACK
Little Black Dress, The LBD Project, Book 1
Red Heels, The LBD Project, Book 2
Lydia, Woman of Purple
Her Most Precious Gift
Shooting Stars Traveling Circus

International Discretionary Intelligence-Gathering Organization

Attn: Max Fischer, Director

Tuesday, May 27

Situation Report, RE: LBD Project, Prototype Field Test

From: Eleanor McKinnon-Grey, InDIGO Agent

Beginning week nine of what was to be a two-week mission. Agents Hedge Parker, Evan Tyler, and Rowan Kirk successfully infiltrated and dismantled an extortion operation headed by Paris Couturier, Anton Hrevic (dec.) and Xandra Yakovsky (in custody), and exposed their connection to fellow InDIGO team member, Jarrett Brawn, leading to his death.

The team consequently followed leads to Marseilles, Barcelona, and London, exposing terror activities related to the aforementioned operations, as well as interference in multiple governments, including personal threats to heads of state and their families. Activities also included intentional disruption of international commerce and resources. Specific situations involved Agent Teo Ramos dismantling explosive devices at multiple sites. His bravery saved the lives of Sec. Douglas Mabry's family, as he sacrificed his life for theirs.

At this date, it is my recommendation that Agent Kirk returns to DC to begin the evaluation process of this mission, and for Agents Parker and Tyler to follow up on remaining leads, the resolution of which will conclude this field test.

I look forward to answering any questions you may have when I return to domestic headquarters in two days.

Respectfully,

E M-G

CHAPTER ONE

Evan Tyler focused on the creased piece of stationery with a butterfly sketched on it. Just a few days earlier, her teammate, Agent Teo Ramos, had made the drawing and then tattooed an identical butterfly in henna on her hip. Now he was dead. She had only a few minutes to write a note to Teo's sister, while the rest of the team rushed to pack their gear.

Dear Mariposa,

My name is Eve, and I was a friend of your brother, Matteo. I met him while we were both backpacking across Europe, and we became close. I am so sorry for your loss. He was a good man with a generous spirit and a strong heart. I was with him at the time of his accident, and I can tell you that he passed instantly and didn't suffer. I am writing this note on a drawing Teo made for me. I know he'd want you to have it. He loved you very much and spoke of you often. He told me several times how proud he was of his beautiful sister. Please know that you are in my prayers.

She wanted to say much more. She wanted to tell Mariposa that her brother died a hero, saving lives every day. Dismantling bombs. Dismantling terrorists of every shape and kind. She wanted to tell her that he faced the worst people in the world and still maintained a positive outlook. That was forbidden. If she dared to write those words, the whole note would be burned. No, better to write words of comfort that Teo's sister would actually receive.

Evan sat in the quiet gray bedroom of the London hotel suite, listening to the rain. A clap of thunder sent a chill down her spine. She folded the note to Teo's sister and slipped it into an envelope from the nearby desk. She checked the room to make sure there was nothing else she needed to give Kirk or Eleanor. Evan's heart ached in every way. She had to say goodbye to Kirk, the man who recruited her into the International Discretionary Intelligence Gathering Organization. He'd been her partner since the very beginning. He was the reason she was in the LBD project. He was the voice in her ear, literally.

And Eleanor. Elle was Evan's inspiration. Tough as nails and honey sweet. She always seemed to know how to gently keep the team in line, but she could hold her own against the powers that be. Evan didn't want the two of them to go, but she knew it was necessary.

In the sitting room, Hedge Parker and Rowan Kirk were discussing how best to track down Costa Alenko, or whatever he might be calling himself these days. Evan took the letter to Elle and waited for her to end her phone conversation.

"That's why we are sending them to Amsterdam," Elle explained. Evan knew she was speaking with the head of InDIGO, Max Fischer. "Yes, Kirk and I will be in Paris this evening and in DC by late tomorrow morning." Elle rolled her gray-green eyes and smiled at Evan. "Yes, sir. And I'll give you that information face to face." Elle didn't wait for more. She clicked off her phone and nodded to Evan. "You have the note?"

Evan handed the envelope to her superior officer. "I kept it short and as truthful as we're allowed."

"She'll appreciate something personal. It's always better than a phone call and a box of ash." Elle took a deep breath and glanced around the room. "Kirk and I are heading out in ten minutes. You two should have your docs and tickets within the hour. Safe travels."

The tension in the room was an invisible fog, penetrating everything and everyone. The team was down one. Evan knew that the others must be hurting as much as she was, but no one said anything. Evan glanced through the windows to the balcony, desperate for even the most insignificant interaction. "You don't think the rain will cause any delays, do you?"

Elle shook her head. "No, this is London. If rain were a factor, they'd never get a plane off the ground." All business.

Hedge and Evan walked Elle and Kirk to the door of the suite. Evan felt a knot growing in her stomach. She hated goodbyes, but this time she was sure the knot was forming in anticipation of being alone with Hedge. This last week had been a rollercoaster for them. She wasn't sure what was coming next.

Hedge shook hands with Elle and then with Kirk. Evan followed his lead. She watched as her friends walked to the elevator and then disappeared behind the sliding brass doors. *Deep breath.* Evan turned to face her team leader, making the mistake of looking directly into his midnight blue eyes. Words failed her.

She wished she could collapse into him and cry for the next hour. That she didn't even have to say the words. That he'd comfort her. That he'd let her comfort him. But that was forbidden, too.

"Will you be ready to go when our papers arrive?" Hedge asked.

Evan wondered if he was as anxious as she was. He looked as cool as ever. At six-foot-four, he stood only a little taller than her. He was standing closer than she expected, and she could smell his aftershave. Herbal and woodsy. She tilted her head back a fraction of an inch. "I'm ready now." She blinked when she heard her own voice. Her words sounded breathy and completely inappropriate. They reflected how she felt, but not how she was supposed to feel.

Hedge didn't seem to notice. He turned away from her and toward the windows again. "Kirk says our contact in Amsterdam will meet us first thing in the morning."

Evan released a long slow breath and nodded. "That will give us time to review and maybe get a little rest."

Neither spoke as they moved their luggage to the door and

scanned the suite for anything left behind. Hedge took a towel from the bathroom and wiped down the two bedrooms and the kitchenette, removing all traceable fingerprints

Once he completed his task, he started his routine of pacing. From the entry door to the sofa and back. Evan checked herself in the mirror by the door, applying one more coat of cinnamon lipstick. She tugged at the hem of the Little Black Dress she wore and then turned to look over her shoulder to make sure the back was straight. Her high-tech couture was powered down. The notebook that monitored it was packed away in Hedge's leather carry-on bag. For now, it was just a dress.

She considered how easy it would be to use it to her advantage. She could slink to Hedge's side and ask him to look her over. She could push her bare shoulders back and bite her lip. She could raise the hem on the dress and flash her legs. She could do all the things that Hedge liked. But she wouldn't. She couldn't. She wasn't going to manipulate him anymore.

She pulled on her green cardigan, pushing the sleeves up for a casual look, camouflaging the cocktail dress into daywear. As she finished securing the last button on her sweater, her phone rang. She raised her brows high when she saw who was calling.

"Hi, Daddy!" Evan's voice chirped.

Hedge spun around to face her.

"Hey, Punkin' Pie. A little bird told me you might be in London. And it just so happens that I am, too. Can your old man take you to dinner tonight?" Gordon Tyler asked.

Evan frowned. "Oh, Daddy, I can't. I'm on a flight out this evening. I'm actually about to leave for the airport right now."

"No worries, darling. Can I meet you somewhere on your way? I just want a hug from my baby girl. That's not too much to ask."

Evan looked at Hedge and made a pretty-please pout with

her lips before she realized what she was doing. She turned away from him and drew another deep breath. "I think I can make that happen. Can you be at Piccadilly Circus in thirty minutes?"

Hedge marched around the room to face her, shaking his head in a fervent *no*.

Evan turned away again as Gordon agreed.

"Great! I'll see you there." Evan dropped her phone into her purse and took a slow turn to face Hedge. "It's my dad. It would be weird if I refused to see him while we're both in the same place."

Hedge huffed. "You could have told him that you've already left London." He crossed his arms over his chest and frowned.

Evan shook her head. "My daddy knows what I do. He's the one person I can always be honest with. It's hard to lie to him."

"If he knows what you do, then he understands when you do have to lie." Hedge's chin wrinkled in a way Evan hadn't noticed before when he had his goatee. "And he's not the only person you can be honest with."

Evan tilted her head and took a step toward him. "Can I please just have five minutes with my dad on the way to the airport? I promise I won't ask for any more favors." She waited for an answer but got little more than a hard stare in response. "If I can be honest with you, then you'll understand when I tell you that I'm hurting and I do need a hug from my daddy right now."

It wasn't manipulation. It was true. She didn't pout or pose. He asked for honesty, and she gave it to him.

"Five minutes." Hedge sighed; his tone softened. "I know you're hurting."

Evan nodded. Maybe this honesty thing wasn't so bad. Maybe she could tell him how she felt. It was never a question of attraction between them. It was always about doing the job without emotional interference. Hedge's track record hadn't been too good on that point, as Evan understood it. But maybe it would be different with them.

"I …." Evan was cut short by a knock at the door.

With one hand positioned to draw his sidearm, Hedge approached the door and looked through the peephole. "Yes?"

"Package for you," said a voice from the hall.

"I didn't order anything." Hedge recited his line.

"It's from your grandmother." The correct answer.

Hedge relaxed his shoulders and opened the door. The young man gave him a large envelope and nodded. "There's a car downstairs now."

Hedge thanked him and then turned back to Evan. "Let's go."

Evan grabbed her red roller bag and purse and followed Hedge to the elevator. She was going to see her daddy.

CHAPTER TWO

Evan stared out the window of the black SUV as Hedge maneuvered through the narrow London streets leading to the famous Piccadilly roundabout. "I forget to look around sometimes." Evan's gaze jumped from one building to the next. "At the city, I mean. In the last four weeks, we've been in Paris, Marseilles, Barcelona, and London. Some of the most beautiful places in the world, and I've barely noticed." She took a few seconds to appreciate all the people crowding the famous intersection of four major streets. Evan turned to the southeast side of the Circus, where a breathtaking bronze sculpture of Anteros rose over the octagonal Shaftesbury Fountain.

"Too busy studying faces and features to look up. It's what we all do." Hedge pointed to the monument ahead of them. "I'll make the loop. When you see your father, let me know. I'll slow down enough for you to jump." He smiled at her from the corner of his mouth.

Evan scanned the faces of everyone moving around the Circus. "At least the rain has let up for a minute." Then she saw him. Sitting on a folded newspaper on a step at the base of the fountain. Brown suit, gray shirt, gray tie. He had a little more silver at his temples than the last time Evan saw him, but the smile was the same.

"Lemme out here," she said. She had the door open and was nearly on the curb before Hedge brought the vehicle to a stop.

"I was just kidding about jumping," he said. "I'll be right back here in five."

Evan waved and hurried up the steps and into the broad wingspan of her father's arms. She inhaled the familiar combination of unsmoked cigars and Old Spice.

"Hey, Punkin' Pie." He kissed her cheek before releasing their embrace. "I missed you." He gestured to the step where he'd been waiting, unfolded the paper for more space, and they both sat. "London has been in the news for a few days. Any of that you?" he asked.

"Daddy, you know better." Evan swept their surroundings with a glance. Couples taking photos everywhere. Selfies, group shots, video, panoramas. She guessed that in the five minutes she'd spend here, she'd probably end up in a few hours worth of video and hundreds of photos.

Her dad nodded. "I thought probably so."

"How's Momma?" Evan hoped to shift the conversation.

"She's good. Probably redecorating a room or two while I'm gone. I swear, every time I come home from a trip, there's more pink.

Evan laughed. "Sounds like Momma. So what brings you to London, Daddy?" She leaned against his shoulder with hers. "You have another consulting job?"

He raised his thick brow. "Yeah, with this summit thing going on, a couple of clients asked if I might help them work out a little deal. Oil tycoons. Everyone is in one place, so it seemed convenient enough."

Evan caught a slight strain in his voice. Something she hadn't heard in a long time. "Are you okay, Dad?"

"Sure, honey. Don't worry about me. I just wanted to see your pretty face while I had the chance."

Evan sat back and blinked. "That sounds a little final. What's going on?"

Gordon cocked his head and sighed. "I just meant that you and I are in the same city at the same time. That doesn't happen often. I just wanted to take advantage of that coincidence."

Evan nodded and reached out for his hand. A nearby car backfired, and as it did, both Evan and her father ducked their heads, nearly bumping them together. It was an automatic reflex to anything that sounded like gunfire. As Evan raised her head back up, she realized that Gordon had the same reaction.

"Daddy, really. What's going on?"

Gordon shrugged and seemed to look more somber. He knit his brows together and lowered his voice. "It's probably nothing. I mean, that just now was an old reflex from my army days. But I've been a little more on edge, I guess. I can tell you— you, more than anyone, know how to keep a secret." He glanced from one side to another. "My oil tycoons, the ones I'm working with on this trip, happen to be Russia and the EU, as well as a little side deal with the UK."

"What?" Evan compressed her gasp into a whisper. She knew her dad often used his connections in the Middle East and Texas for consulting with civilian contractors, but she'd never known him to negotiate deals between countries. Certainly not with Russia.

"Don't panic. There's nothing illegal about it." Gordon squared his shoulders as a light rain began again. "I'm actually there to make sure it's all on the up-and-up."

Evan released a deep breath. "I didn't think you were doing anything illegal." Evan glanced up to see Hedge pulling up to the curb in front of them. "But there's plenty of legal stuff that's still dangerous. Are you working with good people? No, or you wouldn't be on edge."

Gordon grimaced. "It's fine. Not dangerous at all. I'm just a little rusty." He nodded toward the black SUV. "Do you like your team? Y'all getting on well?"

Evan smirked at his subject change. "I do, and we are."

Evan's dad leaned forward and kissed her forehead. "Good. That's what a man wants for his baby girl. Now, you gotta get back to work and so do I. I'll call you when I get a chance and let you know how it all works out."

Evan sighed. "How long will you be in London?"

"I'm here for another three or four days, then in Dallas for two more, then back home." He stood and squeezed her hand as she stood beside him. "Speaking of home—" He didn't have to finish his question.

"I'm gonna try to get home for Thanksgiving this year if I can. You give Momma a kiss for me, and tell her I love her."

"I will, Punkin' Pie. And you take care, too. Your momma is counting on Thanksgiving, and you know I don't like lying to her about you." Gordon squeezed her into another hug and then turned to face Regent Street. Looking over his shoulder at her, he said, "I love you, Evan."

"Love you, too, Daddy." Evan studied his fading smile as he turned and walked down the steps and into a crowd at the nearby crosswalk. Her stomach tightened as the light rain continued. She picked up the newspaper from where they'd been sitting. The headline read *Global Energy Summit Begins*. She looked again to see a photo of Michael Cooper below the fold, with a smaller heading announcing his tragic death. *Tragic.*

She used the paper to cover her hair as she darted through the rain to the SUV. Hedge pushed the door open for her, and she jumped inside.

"Let's go." Evan shivered as a few icy drops of water filtered through her hair and down the back of her neck.

"Your father seems nice." Hedge turned the vehicle into traffic and headed west toward the airport. Evan silently stared out the window. "Hey, you okay?"

Evan nodded. "He seemed like something was bothering him."

"A little distracted?" Hedge asked.

"Yeah," Evan said with a tired sigh. "I guess he knows what he's doing, though."

Hedge shrugged. "I hope so. Negotiating deals between world powers can get tricky."

Evan whipped her head around to face Hedge. "Did you listen in on my conversation?"

Hedge kept his eyes straight ahead. "We're on the job."

"But that was a *private* conversation. That was five minutes of personal time. You were not invited." Evan crossed her arms and frowned. "I can't believe you were listening."

Hedge chuffed. "It was five minutes. And it wasn't like you were talking about private matters."

"Yes, we were." Evan furrowed her brow and balled her fists.

"Thanksgiving?" Hedge tightened his grip on the steering wheel.

"It *was* a private conversation." She glared at the side of his head. She could feel her face flushing red as her heart pounded in her ears.

"You didn't disconnect your ear receiver. I assumed you didn't care if I heard." Hedge shook his head.

Evan noticed him glancing at her from the side of his eye. "I never had to disconnect with Kirk. He just *knew* not to listen."

"Well, in case you haven't noticed, I'm not your precious Kirk." Hedge growled as a car cut in front of him and braked abruptly. "I'm not perfect like him. I'm still trying to figure this thing out."

Evan gasped. This wasn't fair. She knew Kirk wasn't perfect, and she shouldn't expect Hedge to fall into his place without a little bit of a learning curve. Evan thought about when she first had the receiver implanted in her ear canal. About how long it had taken Kirk and her to figure when he'd listen and when she had time to herself. She decided to concede.

"I should— " they both started at the same time.

Evan grimaced. "I shouldn't have snapped at you. We just need time to work this out."

Hedge lowered his chin. "I shouldn't have listened in. Since we haven't had time to work everything out, I should have known you needed a private moment."

Evan shook her head and took a deep breath. "We can work out nuances later. Let's please not argue now."

"Agreed." Hedge nodded. He leaned forward to look up at the darkening sky. "This rain is getting worse. I hope it doesn't mess with our flight."

Weather? Fantastic. How can I make this relationship work? I swing between wanting to pull his shirt off and kiss him to wanting to punch his lights out. And the best we can do is talk about the weather. Evan couldn't stand the idea. She wanted more.

"He did sound distracted, didn't he?" She turned in her seat to face Hedge. "And I don't like the idea of him being at this summit thing. Too much trouble with that already."

Hedge nodded. "He's retired army? Doing the civilian contractor thing, right?"

"Yes. When he first retired, my dad worked for an oil company outside of Houston. He had connections in the Middle East and all over the world. I suppose he's qualified to do what he does." Evan laughed to herself. "But then again, Daddy can talk jus' about anybody into anything."

Hedge laughed. "That's where you get it, then." He sighed.

Evan guessed that he felt as relieved as she did. "He ducked at that backfire like he was dodging bullets."

"You did, too."

"Yes, but I've actually had people shooting at me in the

last two weeks." She worried about her dad. "Do you think he's suffering from PTSD?"

"It's not uncommon, and it would be a reasonable assumption if he saw much combat." Hedge frowned at the slower pace of traffic as they neared Heathrow Airport. "I hate driving in London," he muttered.

Evan patted his shoulder. "You're doing fine. And we're not late. Just breathe." She kept her tone calm and even, though her stomach was still tight. She realized she was pushing hard on the invisible brake in front of her. She had hoped a hug from Daddy would make her feel better.

It didn't.

CHAPTER THREE

After a three-hour delay at Heathrow, Hedge and Evan were finally aboard their plane to Amsterdam. Hedge breathed heavily and stretched after the fasten-seatbelts light went off. His hip wound was healing, but he couldn't get comfortable in economy seating, even on a short flight.

He wrestled with his conscience, too. Maybe he should apologize to Evan, after listening in on her private conversation. On the other hand, he didn't like coincidences, and there were too many to ignore. Her father *just happens* to be in London, and he's dealing with the countries and the markets that they were focusing on with their mission. And he asked specifically if she was involved in the events making headlines. He didn't like it.

But then again, where else in the world would his business take him, other than a global energy summit? And Evan is his daughter; of course, he would ask about her. It was perfectly natural for him to want to talk to her or take her to dinner, more so after hearing about bombs and suspicious deaths. He knew what Evan did. What she faced every day. *Focus, man!*

It was time to get some work done. Now was their chance to review the files on Kirk's notebook. They had a buffer of empty seats around them, courtesy of Elle, giving them the freedom to discuss their mission with a certain degree of privacy.

Hedge opened the file with Kirk's spreadsheet of notes on the ongoing situation. He turned the small computer to face Evan. "Let's go over what we know so far." He nodded as she focused on the screen, but then saw her eyes glaze.

Evan grimaced and then shifted the laptop back to face Hedge. "Great. And you can add to his notes as we go."

Hedge frowned. The spreadsheet was in some kind of

shorthand. He could make out the names easily enough. AH would be Anton Hrevic. XY for Xandra Yakovsky. NA was Nastya Alenko, and so forth. After that, the notes became a little sketchy. He turned the screen back to Evan. "I'll let you add to Kirk's notes. Better to keep it all consistent."

Evan laughed. "Do I look like a girl who reads spread-sheets?"

Hedge made eye-contact, after avoiding it all day. Evan's face, even filled with worry and frustration, was magazine per-fect. *Who looks like this in person?* Her lips were pursed and full and cocked just slightly to one side. Her cheeks flushed. Her brows arched. But her eyes. Evan's eyes flashed a deep teal like the blue-green ripples in the Mediterranean Sea. He saw the worry, but behind it, he saw determination.

"You look like a woman capable of doing anything you set your mind to." Hedge smiled, triggering a smile in return.

"Awh, that's adorable." Evan shook her head and shrugged. "This just looks like a bunch of initials and numbers to me. I don't know how to read it."

Hedge frowned. "But Kirk was your partner for years. You never learned to read his notes?"

"I didn't have to. I had Kirk with me." Evan sighed. She slumped back in her seat. "Have you been keeping notes?"

Hedge closed the notebook. "Not much. Kirk had us covered. When Elle and I were out in the field, I kept sticky notes on a wall. It's old-school, but I guess we can make that work when we get to our room." He saw Evan's face brighten. "Do you have any sticky notes?"

"Yep." She dug into her purse and retrieved a stack of neon green paper squares. "Let's start now."

Hedge pulled a pen from his breast pocket and clicked the end as he handed it to her, feeling the softness and warmth of her hand.

He nodded. "We know that Anton was working for some-one else. Brawn, too. Xandra, Nastya, Cooper—we don't know what tier they are on. They could be working for an individual, an agency, or a government."

Evan wrote quickly, flipping the note paper with each new idea. She looked up with a spark in her expression. "And Costa Alenko, too. Is he pulling strings or just a puppet?"

This was what Hedge loved. He felt the electricity surge. He loved the chemistry they had together, but it scared him, too. It would be easy to get personal. She wanted it as much as he did. But letting her in was dangerous. For her and for him.

He'd been there before. He'd been told to stand down and walk away. He hadn't been able to do it. He couldn't leave Elle in the field to die. He didn't.

Hedge looked up at Evan, realizing it was already too late. He wouldn't leave her either, no matter what orders he was given or by whom. He was in deep, and he knew it.

Hedge nodded. "Let's look at the government angle, or at least a government agency. There's a lot going on here that would be tough for an individual to pull off."

Evan clicked the pen a few times. "Not impossible, but definitely difficult. And let's not forget that Xandra said that she was *going to be* the Empress of Russia or some such a thing."

Hedge chuffed. "Xandra is a lunatic."

Evan nodded with enthusiasm. "Oh, she's definitely crazy, but someone has her convinced that it will happen. She's not stu-pid. She's expecting some huge upheaval in the Russian govern-ment or hierarchy."

Hedge drummed his fingers on the closed laptop. "With that in mind, I'd surmise it's not the official Russian government orchestrating this. Possibly a shadow organization."

"Maybe even a dark version of the KGB, I mean, the FSB?"

Evan scrawled another note.

"Maybe. But why bother with the global economy and mess with the gold standard? It's got to be bigger than Russia." Hedge looked over her shoulder at her precise cursive. "Nice."

"Yeah, it seems like an awful lot of trouble just to flip Russia. They've already caused upset and instigated change in too many other places." Evan tapped the pen on her bottom lip. "Unless this is a smokescreen. It could be a play to keep eyes looking everywhere but Russia while they work from the inside out."

"So far, all our players are Russian, though. I don't want to discount that idea. It may be spot-on, but we also might be missing a much bigger picture." He watched as she nodded again, moving the pen from her lip to the notepaper.

"Good point." Evan looked up and smiled. At least some of the worry had faded from her eyes.

He almost didn't want to vocalize his next idea. "Michael Cooper was using his assets to keep this scheme going."

Evan didn't seem to blink at the name. "You're right. In the same way that Xandra was paying off people with her gemstones, Cooper was using his cash to fund their organization. The auction purchase was most certainly either a payoff or a laundering transaction."

Hedge was relieved at her nonchalance. He knew Evan's infatuation for Cooper had turned to hate and disgust. She had called him *Cooper* instead of *Michael*. Good. But now Hedge needed forgiveness. He'd advised Evan to do whatever was necessary to turn Cooper. He'd been clear enough. And he had seen the hurt in her expression when he gave her those instructions.

"Hedge?" Evan nudged him, startling him back to attention. "What are you thinking?"

He was tempted to tell her. "I was just thinking that Cooper's money went somewhere. We need to track that account down and find out whose name is on it."

"Or names."

Hedge pressed his fingers over the cover of the laptop to resist his urge to take her hands in his. "Kirk may already have that information for us. We can check in with him as soon as we get settled in our hotel."

Evan clicked the pen a few times. "I've never been to Amsterdam before. Are you gonna take me to see some tulips?"

Hedge smiled at her easy innocence. "Nope. We're about a month late for the tulips. And our accommodations are closer to the red-light district than to the flowers. But the architecture is remarkable. I'd be happy to give you a tour of some historical cathedrals."

Evan leaned in and sighed. Hedge thought she might kiss him, and he debated for a split-second whether to resist or not. She only smiled and blinked. "Have you been to every city in the world, Hedge Parker?"

He laughed and let his shoulders relax. "I haven't, but sometimes I think my list of places-I've-been is longer than my list of places-still-to-go."

Evan tilted her head and raised one brow. "And, of course, you speak Dutch fluently?"

Hedge nodded, almost embarrassed by his gift for linguistics. "I can hold a decent conversation."

"I suppose if we're gonna be partners, you're gonna have to help me train my tongue."

Hedge almost choked at the suggestion.

Before he could respond, Evan stammered out a correction. "With learning other languages. You know what I mean. You have a dirty mind."

Hedge shook his head. "I didn't say anything."

"You should be grateful my daddy isn't here for this conversation."

And with that one remark, Hedge watched the worry return to Evan's eyes. He reached out and took the pen from between her fingers and cupped her chilled hands in his. "He knows how to take care of himself, you know."

Evan nodded, and Hedge watched as she pulled a silent shadow over herself like a hood.

He squeezed her hand. "Listen, we'll track down our man, save the world, and have you home for Thanksgiving and you and your dad can swap stories during the game."

Evan laughed, but without a sparkle in her eye. Hedge slipped the pen back into his pocket as the fasten-seat-belts light dinged overhead. "We're almost there." He tucked the laptop and paperwork into his leather carry-on and stowed it for landing. "Did I tell you that we're staying in a really nice hotel instead of a dump?"

Evan shook her head and smiled. "That will be a nice change."

Hedge agreed. Apparently, Elle felt they could use a break from the run-down flats with whining elevators and de-flated mattresses. "The building used to belong to a newspaper printers. Still has the printer theme. Very trendy. Food is sup-posed to be good, too."

"Have you stayed there before?" Evan rolled her head back, stretching her neck.

"No. But I'm looking forward to it." He didn't want to tell her that he and Elle had planned a stay at the INK hotel, but when she was injured in the field, everything changed. Just one more reason not to become personally involved with a partner.

Evan seemed to read his expression, too. She took Hedge's hand again. "I know we've both been through a lot in the last few weeks. I'm hurting, and I know you are, too. But whatever comes up. Whatever it is. I have your back. Just like I know you have mine."

Hedge sighed. This was what he wanted. Could he—could they—make it work? They were good together as partners. They weren't afraid of each other. *Well, maybe he was a little afraid of her.* He smiled. *But more than that?* He was sure she could do better. He was also sure that he never would.

Turbulence rocked the plane as it broke through a layer of clouds. Below the white wisps, the city stretched out below them in a spider-web shape, striped with channels of water coming in at precise angles.

Hedge leaned over Evan to look out the small airplane window. He could smell the perfume in her hair. He felt the warmth of her skin without touching any more than her hands. *This is business. This is the job. This is what he lived for. This is what he loved.*

He found himself looking directly into her clear blue eyes. His heart thumped heavy in his chest. *This is what he loved.*

CHAPTER FOUR

Hedge and Evan maneuvered through the low-ceilinged maze of the Schiphol terminal, past the over-lit locker area where a screaming child had lost sight of his mother for a split second, and into the long corridor to the taxi pick-up.

Evan was grateful that her long legs were able to keep pace with Hedge's meter-length strides. They didn't even attempt the moving walkways, which were crowded with exhausted passengers resting up after nine or so hours over the Atlantic. They flew past the tourists and flight crews and hurried out to the curb.

Elle had ordered a limo to pick them up and take them to the INK Hotel at the center of the city. They hopped into the sedan and settled in to enjoy the ride. The car took them through streets lined with thousands of bicycles parked row after row in front of tall brick buildings that sat too close to the road. After several minutes, their car approached the Royal Palace and turned left in front of it. They passed the Nieuwe Kerk, and Hedge commented on the architecture.

"This cathedral is called the new church." Hedge gestured to the spires and stained-glass windows that seem to decorate every inch of the building.

Evan leaned forward to look out her window. "I'm assuming new is a relative term?"

Hedge laughed. "Yeah. This building is from the 15th century. The old church, a few blocks from here, is from the 13th century."

Evan grinned and sat back in her seat. "All of these buildings seem old and new at the same time. I suppose everything is relative."

Their car pulled to the curb to let them out in front of an old orange-brick printing house, now a boutique hotel punctuated with arches lined in cut stone. Hedge got out, paid the driver, and opened Evan's door for her. He followed her through the hotel's entry and into the atrium-like lobby.

A very tall and slim man greeted them at the front desk, and within a few seconds, Hedge had the room keys.

"Third floor," he said to Evan. "Our lucky number."

They entered the sleek elevator carriage and waited for the doors to close. As the car ascended, Evan raised one eyebrow. "Déjà vu. At least this elevator has had some maintenance in this century."

Hedge's phone rang before they reached their floor. "Yeah," he answered. He listened and frowned and clicked off as the doors opened. He took Evan's arm, and they hurried together to the room. "Drop your stuff. Take off your sweater, and I'll power up the dress. We have to go right now."

Before Evan had the chance to argue, her phone buzzed in her hand. "Hello?"

"Did you get my message? We must meet right away," and then the line went dead.

Evan nodded to Hedge and shrugged. "All right then. I guess we gotta go." She pulled off her green cardigan, brushed out her red tresses, and put on a fresh coat of lipstick. Once they got the laptop on and the dress operational, she followed Hedge back to the elevator. "What about a car?"

"We shouldn't need one. We can walk to our meet from here."

Evan followed Hedge past the thin concierge and out onto the street. They walked south past the new church and then across the street to the palace. On the other side of the palace, Hedge led them left another three blocks to a bridge over the canal. Once across the water, the two headed north once again.

It didn't take long before Evan realized where they were—the Red Light District. Professionals and their pimps stood in front of shops with suggestive names like Pure Lust and Sexy Amsterdam.

"You've got to be kidding me." Evan eyed one woman wearing a bright blue spandex micro-mini and 6-inch platform heels. "Why do our contacts always want to meet in places like this?" Now she knew why Hedge wanted her to take off the sweater.

Hedge grinned from ear to ear. "Says the woman in the cocktail dress at four in the afternoon." He pushed out his elbow, and Evan grabbed it. Once she was closer, he lowered his voice. "It's places like this that don't draw attention."

"I guess." She adjusted her strut to match her cover. Sexy redhead in a little black dress and red stiletto heels, on the arm of a tall, handsome businessman. Not ideal, but okay.

Another block, another bridge. This one was for pedestrians, and it was loaded to capacity. They walked another 50 meters and stopped in their tracks. Just ahead they saw flashing lights and half a dozen police officers roping off the scene.

"This does not bode well," Hedge said under his breath.

The couple moved slowly to the front of the crowd to see what had happened. Behind two officers, Evan could see a bright orange tarp covering something in the street. An older man wearing an official-looking blue suit pulled a corner of the cover back for a second, shook his head and dropped it over the face of the dead man. Evan knew instantly. It was their guy, and he'd been shot point-blank.

Hedge didn't wait for an explanation. He turned them both around and headed back to the iron bridge directly behind them. They crossed to the other side of the canal and into a narrow passage between buildings. Hedge untucked his shirt to cover his pistol, removed his jacket, and handed it to Evan. "Put this on and roll up the sleeves."

Evan did and then reached into her handbag and pulled out a hair band. Within a few seconds, her red hair was knotted at the nape of her neck. "You prefer the sexy secretary look?"

"Don't make jokes. That could've been us."

"Yessir," Evan said. "What now?"

Hedge looked back to the street and then over his left shoulder. He pointed to Evan's chest. "In the jacket's left breast pocket is a black wallet. I need it."

Evan reached in and retrieved a black leather badge holder and handed it to her partner. "Who are we today?"

"Detectives, I guess. Who else would be on the scene so quickly?" Hedge looked her over for a second and then nodded. "Do you have something for taking notes?"

"Of course." She pulled out a small notepad and pen.

Hedge placed his hand on her lower back and led her to the black arched front doors of the ancient cathedral in front of them. He looked up and jutted his chin toward the roof on either side. Evan saw them. The old church, or Oude Kerk as all the signs read, was peppered with security cameras covering every angle of the area.

"This will be easier than trying to catch all the video from the tourists' cell phones."

Evan agreed and followed him through the front doors. A young woman greeted them just inside. "Mag ik u helpen?" she asked.

Hedge nodded and a stream of Dutch rolled off his tongue. The woman directed them to a small room at the back of the building. Hedge flashed his badge to a security guard sitting in front of a dozen monitors. Within a minute or two they were studying video of the fatal encounter on the street.

To the security guard, it appeared to be no more than a

cursory review, but Evan was using her dress to capture all of the information from the video surveillance cameras. In a matter of minutes, they had everything they needed. They thanked the guard and left.

"We should get back to the room before whoever did this starts looking for us." Hedge led them back to the hotel using a different route.

Evan kept close watch of where they were going and of every person they passed along the way. Before reentering their hotel, Evan pulled the band from her hair and combed her fingers through the loose curls. She pushed the cuffs out of the sleeves of Hedge's jacket and returned it to him. Inside they smiled at the porter and asked for a menu for the night.

Back in their room, Evan quickly changed into casual clothes and handed the dress over to Hedge. He plugged it into its charging bag and booted up the laptop to see what they captured on video.

"Shouldn't we call Elle?" Evan sank into the sofa next to Hedge.

He frowned and shook his head. "Not until I have something definite to tell her. Why don't you look up our contact's information and we can make a few calls later."

Evan nodded. "I'll get right on that." She gestured to the laptop. "This will take a second. You should change into something more comfortable, and I'll order dinner."

Hedge smirked at her. "I'll order after I change. Start reviewing the videos and let me know if you see something."

Evan tapped at the keyboard for a second, and the first video started playing. Evan stopped it when she realized that it was pointing the wrong direction. She began the next video and fast forwarded until the timestamp reached just a few minutes before they arrived on the scene. She saw her contact speaking with two men on the bridge in front of the church. The first man wore a hat and was careful to keep his face hidden from the cameras. The second man was not so careful, and Evan's heart began to pound when she recognized him.

The video feed was jumpy, and the color was dull, but the brown suit and gray shirt were clear enough. The hair. The build. But it couldn't be him. Evan had left him in London and went straight to the airport. How was it possible for him to get to Amsterdam before them?

And he wasn't going to Amsterdam. He said he would be in London for a few days. It couldn't be him. She watched a few seconds more and then paused the video. It was grainy, and the reflecting sunlight from the canal caused a glare at the bottom of the screen. It was impossible.

She advanced the picture one frame at a time to be sure. Her ears were ringing as adrenaline pumped through her whole body. Her fingers were shaking on the computer keys. She couldn't blink.

The three men argued. That was evident. Their contact reached into his pocket, for a weapon, she suspected. The man in the hat kept his head down. He took a step back. The man in the brown suit raised a pistol and aimed at their guy. A white flare of smoke and fire and their man was down. The man in the hat took the other man's arm, and they started walking away. Before they were enveloped by the crowds, the shooter looked back over his shoulder, directly into the camera.

No question. No doubt. Evan had known that face all her life.

"Is that your father?" Hedge asked.

Evan jumped at the sound of his voice. "What do we do now?"

CHAPTER FIVE

"No answer. Straight to voicemail again," Evan said as she scrolled through the icons on her phone. "And no reply to my texts." She pressed her fingertips to her temples and closed her eyes. Why did he lie to her? Why did he come to Amsterdam? What was he really doing in Europe at all—apart from murdering a man who might have had information on their target?

Hedge clicked off his conversation with Elle. "Okay, here's what we know. Your father is in London, or at least, he was in London this morning, to help mediate an oil deal between the EU and Russia. Then a man who looks considerably like your father is seen on security footage murdering our contact just minutes before we are supposed to speak with him."

Evan groaned. "It was my father. It wasn't someone who just looked like him. It was him."

"And you're one hundred percent sure?"

"He was wearing the same clothes as he was this morning. Brown slacks, brown jacket, brown and gray striped shirt, gray necktie. You can even see the tie clip I gave him last Christmas, right there in the video." Evan pointed to the laptop monitor. She could feel her fingertips throbbing, but little else.

Hedge sighed and raked his fingers through his hair. "Eleanor doesn't know anything else about the situation. Or if she does, she's not at liberty to say."

"You asked specifically?"

"No, but I trust her to tell me anything she's allowed to say." He looked back to his phone as if he thought he heard it ring.

"What if it was about me? About my dad?" Evan shook her

head. "She might not tell us everything she knows. We haven't always kept her in the loop on every move we've made."

"What are you suggesting?"

"Not that she's keeping us in the dark out of spite, not that." Evan stood up and walked to the window. She looked down at the hundreds of people walking, driving, and bicycling by. None of them seemed to care that just a few blocks away a man was murdered. Evan collected her thoughts before she continued. "I just wonder if she would keep information from us if she thought we might take matters into our own hands."

"She knows we're not stupid," Hedge said.

"That's what I mean." Evan faced him. "She might think we would go hunting for him."

Hedge reached for her hand. "Wouldn't you want to?"

"Yes." Evan walked to him and dropped her head onto his chest. He quickly closed his arms around her. For the first time in three days, she felt as though she could breathe.

"That's what I figured on." He rested his chin on the top of her head. "I did get her to send me everything she could find on our contact. He was MI-6. His name is Calvin Moss. I got a few aliases, too, including the one he sent us. If you're up for it, I will make some calls—channel my inner Rowan Kirk—and see what we can find about him. He links our current mission with your father, so any lead we find, we'll take."

Evan looked up into his eyes and smiled. "Thank you, Hedge."

He dropped his arms and took a step away. "I'll do some digging on Moss while you make some calls to your dad's associates. Call anyone who might know anything about his business."

"Except my mom." Evan drew a deep breath. "I have never been good at keeping secrets from her. Not without the help of my dad."

"Okay, then. Only call her as a last resort, and then only to see if she's heard from him."

Evan quickly got to work on a list of people to try. One by one she called or messaged his co-workers or closest friends. Her father had told them only that he would be out of town for a week or two. Nothing more. She dialed the number of the last oil company he had worked with.

"Mr. Waxman's office," answered a young woman.

Evan cleared her throat. "Cole Waxman, please." A few seconds later Evan heard the voice of her father's old fishing buddy.

"This is Cole," he said.

"Hello, Cole. This is Evan Tyler. It's so sweet to hear your voice."

"It's great to be heard, Evan. How's my girl?" he said with the sound of a broad smile coming through.

"I'm just fine, sir. Thank you for asking." She paused just enough to catch her breath and give him the opportunity to offer any news before she asked. He didn't. "I was calling to see if you could help me out with something."

"Anything, my dear."

"I'm trying to reach my dad. He told me that he was taking a business trip this week. I spoke to him this morning for a minute, but this afternoon when I tried to call, I couldn't get through. Does he have another phone that he uses for business? Could I get that number from you?" Evan tried not to sound desperate. With the loud pounding of her heart in her ears, she couldn't gauge how she was doing.

"Evan, if your dad has another phone number, I sure don't know it. But it's funny that you called. His little business trip isn't for my company or me. He told me about it but didn't let me in on any details. I was actually calling to see how he was —oh, maybe an hour ago—and couldn't even get his voicemail."

Waxman's voice seemed strained to Evan, but maybe she just imagined it. "Do you think we should be worried?"

Evan quickly responded. "Oh, no. I'm sure he's okay. Probably just busy with one thing or another. Most likely he's let time get away from him, and let his battery run out. You know my dad."

"I suppose so," he said. "Well, when you do catch up with him, would you ask him to give me a call, please?"

"I sure will." A second later she ended the call. She turned to face Hedge, who was scribbling notes on a scrap of paper. She waited for him to finish writing before speaking. "Can we try pinging his phone again?"

Hedge gestured to the laptop. "By all means. Maybe he's turned it back on."

Evan tapped at the keyboard, searching for her father's pin on the map. A notification box popped up saying that his cell signal could not be detected.

"Nothing." Evan sighed. "Next?"

Hedge checked his pistol and then stowed it into the band at his lower back. "You wanna try to sleep, or would you rather get out and see what we can find tonight?"

Evan perked up and grabbed her Springfield. "Do we know where we are going? Do we have a way to get there?"

"Everything on our guy Moss says he kept a flat a few miles from here. I'll call a car, and we can check the place out. This late we shouldn't have to worry about police or landlords." Hedge tapped on his ear. "Let's check your com."

Evan nodded and went to the bedroom to pick up her purse. She kept her voice low. "Have you discussed any of this with Elle yet?"

She heard Hedge's breath before his voice. She felt a shiver run down her spine as she listened to the gravel in his tone. "Not yet. I'll give her a call in the morning. There's a time difference, you know?"

Evan was still getting used to the sound of Hedge through her auditory implant instead of Kirk, who had been the voice in her head for the last year. Kirk had always been soft-spoken and fuzzy. Hedge's voice had a whiskey-sharp bite. Evan couldn't decide which she preferred.

She did some quick calculating in her head, as she rejoined him in the living area. "We're hours ahead of her in Virginia. If you wait 'til morning, she'll still be asleep."

"I know." Hedge winked at her.

"Mean."

Hedge and Evan went downstairs and caught their ride to a more residential area of Amsterdam. The small apartment complex was little more than a brick box with windows. There was no charm like all of the buildings in their part of town. Across the narrow street from the building was a small park, flanked on either side with tiny shops and restaurants. Down the road Evan could see tight rows of houses rising behind black street lamps.

Most of the shops were closed, but the restaurants still had lights flickering in the windows. Hedge waved some cash at the driver and gave him instructions to pick them up in an hour at the same location. They got out and walked to the apartment building.

Evan tried the door, which was locked securely. Hedge took a step between her and the street, and within a few seconds she had picked the lock, and they were in the stale-smelling vestibule. Hedge found the post boxes and only 2B had no name label. They nodded to each other and headed up the vinyl-tiled stairs.

Another lock to pick, and they stood in the middle of Moss's flat. It was empty, which didn't surprise either of them.

"Who do you think cleaned it out?" Evan asked.

"Probably Her Majesty's men. I just wonder if anyone else has been here." Hedge closed the blinds before turning off his flashlight and turning on the dull, overhead light.

The room looked even barer with the light on. There was a brown tweed sofa that apparently turned out to a bed. In front of the kitchenette stood a table with two plastic folding chairs on either side. A partition wall divided the main room with a miniature bathroom, containing nothing that wasn't bolted down except for a torn shower curtain.

Hedge opened the small refrigerator to find it empty. Even the plastic ice tray was empty. "Not a trace of him—or anyone for that matter."

"It's too late to canvas neighbors," Evan said.

Hedge pulled back the blind from the one window. "Maybe not." He pointed to the street below.

Evan peered down at the street and saw several people gathered in front of the closest restaurant. She looked up and down the road. "There are at least a dozen people down there and only two cars. All those folks are local."

Hedge raised his eyebrows and smiled at her. "You're quick."

"What are we waiting for? I'm hungry." She led him down the stairs and out into the yellow glow of the street lights.

They smiled at the small group of men smoking in front of the cafe. Hedge greeted them in Dutch, but the men's gaze never left Evan.

"Did your friends forget something?" the tallest man asked in an Irish brogue. He wore a sleeveless T-shirt with a surfboard printed across the front.

"What do you mean?" Evan asked with a broad smile and a lilt in her voice.

The other men laughed and nudged each other.

Surfer flicked his cigarette to the road. "I was probably Mozzy's best friend. Maybe the only one he had here—save the birds he would bring back occasionally. Never had anyone up to his flat in three months. This afternoon his place is packed with people coming and going. And then you two show up after the rest of the crew is out. I figure they forgot something and you were sent to collect it." He looked Evan over carefully.

She shifted her weight toward Hedge, hoping that would be enough to show who was the Alpha in the group, but Surfer didn't take the hint.

"Can I buy you a drink, lovely?" he asked her. "Maybe I have whatever you're looking for."

"Did you talk to Mozzy often?" she asked, not turning down his offer, but not accepting, either. "You were friends?"

"Yeah, we talked every morning. We told each other about our nightly adventures, and then our plans for the day." He scratched at his ribcage and then dug in his shorts pocket for another cigarette. "Let me buy you a drink."

Evan raised and lowered her lashes several times to keep his attention on her eyes. "Did Mozzy say where he was going today?" She bit her lip and took a deep breath, emphasizing her hourglass figure.

"Yeah, yeah, lovely. He tells me he's got to meet a man over in the Red Light. Not that you know about that. You got too much class for that."

Evan tilted her chin down and pursed her lips into a pout. "That's all?"

Surfer took a step toward her and put his hand on her shoulder. "He says he's making a big play today. Gonna land him in a pile of Euros if it goes off. Meeting with a broker, he says." Surfer's voice was barely above a whisper in Evan's ear, but that was more than enough for Hedge to hear.

"A broker?" Evan placed her hand over Surfer's. She wanted him to think she was flirting back. She was actually preparing to break his wrist, if necessary.

"That's what he called him, the Broker. You really are a beauty, aren't you?"

Evan smiled. "The Broker, then. And he was going to set Mozzy up with a load of cash?"

"Come on, lovely, just one drink. You ditch your sailor, and I'll take care of you for tonight." Surfer moved his hand down her back. Before his fingers got too close to her pistol, she took another step nearer Hedge.

"You want to buy my sister a drink?" Hedge took a step toward the man and broadened his stance. "You should ask me for permission."

Surfer finally took a moment to appraise Hedge. Evan watched the expression on his face change from nearly inebriated to adequately paranoid. "No, I don't want to make trouble. I was just being friendly. Your sister is very nice. Very pretty. I don't want no trouble."

Hedge nodded and shot a confident glance at all of the men. He took Evan's hand and started to walk away. She stopped short and pulled her phone from her bag.

"I just want to ask one more thing." She opened a picture of the MI-6 agent and showed it to Surfer. "Is this your Mozzy?"

The man squinted to see the photo. "Yeah, lovely. That's the guy." Evan winked at him and closed her album. Her phone's lock screen reset, and Surfer nodded again. "Yeah, and that bloke looks just like Mozzy's pic of the Broker. You know him, too?"

Evan glanced down at the picture on her phone. It was of her parents—her dad's face smiling in the foreground. Her heart sank, and her head started to pound. *What was happening?*

"What have you gotten yourself into, Daddy?" she whispered as they walked back to the cab.

CHAPTER SIX

"Hi, Mama," Evan said, hoping to sound cheerful. "How are you doing?"

Evan's mother seemed excited to have a call from her only child. "Oh, baby, I'm all right as always. My knee's been acting up again, but other than that, all is well. Are you back in Texas?"

"No, Mama, I'm still in Europe looking at all the beautiful new clothes." Evan smiled at Hedge from across the room. Having someone else in the room gave her a measure of calm that she appreciated.

"Well, I bet you're having fun. Do you see anything nice? How's your magazine article coming?"

Evan nodded as if her mother could see her. "Yes, Mama. My article is practically writing itself. There are lots of beautiful styles. And always a few crazy ones, too. Do you need a new scarf? I can send you one." She thought about the Hermes scarf that Xandra made her buy in Paris.

"Oh, heavens to Betsy! I don't need a scarf. I'm in Texas, hon. It's not even summer yet, and we're already hitting the upper eighties."

Evan laughed. "Gracious! Already?" She knew that weather was a safe topic, but she needed to stretch a bit if she was going to get any information. "I had a call from Daddy yesterday. He said his business trip was going real good." Evan glanced up at Hedge, who was stifling a laugh.

"Then you've talked to him since I have." Her mother sounded preoccupied. "Last I spoke to him he was heading to a rural area in France. He said the cell reception would be out for a few days. Evan, can I ask you something?"

"Sure, Mama, what is it?"

"Do you think that painting I did of your grandpa is good enough to go in the front room? Be honest."

Evan sighed. This was one thing she could be honest about. "Yes, of course, it's good enough. It looks just like him."

"Good, because I'm gonna surprise your daddy by redecorating the whole living room."

"Mama, he'll love that." Evan pulled her feet up under her. "Will you have time to get all of that done before he gets back?" She waited to see if her mother had been given a time frame for her father's trip.

"Sure I will. He said he'd be gone two weeks. That still gives me ten days to get it all done." She paused, and Evan worked out the dates in her head. "Oh, baby, I got to let you go. The UPS guy is here with the drapes I ordered. I love you, Evan."

"Love you, too, Mama." As Evan clicked off, Hedge began to laugh. "What? Don't laugh at my mama."

Hedge shook his head. "I'm not laughing at your mother. I'm laughing at you."

"You're mean." She tossed her pen in his direction.

"It's just that the longer you talked to her, the more your accent came out." He picked up her pen and handed it back to her. "It's cute."

"Don't call me cute. I'll kick your butt." Evan raised her eyebrow. "Anyway, I got a little information from her. Dad told me one thing and her something else. Uggh! I have no idea what he's doing."

"First of all, there's a pretty good chance he knew that whatever he'd be doing in Europe would be dangerous, and it's obviously a secret. So far he's given everybody a different story." He took a seat next to her on the sofa.

Evan stared at the picture on her phone, wishing it would ring again with her dad's number on the screen. She could feel the warmth of Hedge's body. "And second of all?"

Hedge cocked his head to the side and smiled. "You're tough, but you couldn't kick my butt if you tried."

Evan narrowed her gaze and let her lips twitch just enough to catch his attention. "Excuse me, but I happen to know that you have a nasty little wound that is still healing on your pretty little butt. I am trained to exploit that type of situation. So, yes I certainly could take you down."

"I guess you're right, in theory. Maybe one day you can try to prove it to me." Hedge leaned his head back and stared at the ceiling for a few seconds. He stretched his arms out in either direction across the back of the couch.

"I thought we were going to keep everything professional. No fraternization." Evan tucked her shoulder into his armpit and rested her head on his chest. "And aren't you still mad at me?"

Hedge flexed his arm back and let his fingertips graze her hair. "I'm not mad at you. You're mad at me." He turned his head so that his chin rested against her forehead.

"What am I mad at you for again?" she asked.

"Because I was listening to your private conversation with your dad."

Evan nodded, patting his chest with her hand. "Oh yeah. But you were just trying to protect me." She wished this would last, but she was sure that in a few minutes Hedge would return to his professional tone and put a few yards between them. She would enjoy his softer side while it lasted.

"I was. And why am I mad at you?" Hedge moved his other hand to the side of her knee as she curled her body up to his.

Evan shrugged. "I don't know. Because I was getting too close to Teo or because I was too close to Cooper? I was manipulative. I wasn't careful enough."

Hedge stiffened and raised Evan's face to meet his. "Stop right there. I was never angry about any of that. Well, maybe a little, but I wasn't mad at you. You did your job, and you did it well."

Evan leaned into his hand against her cheek. Her body ached with worry and exhaustion, but this felt warm and comfortable. Her voice shook. "And people still died."

Hedge nodded. "That's how life is, and you know it. You aren't to blame for that. We can all do everything perfectly right, and sometimes people still get hurt or killed. That's just part of the job. And if you're to blame for anything, I'll blame you for saving my life. Yes, I do have a scar on my hip, but if you hadn't shot Brawn when you did, he'd have killed me. So if you're going to carry anything around with you, carry that."

Evan listened to his words. She felt his breath on her cheeks and heard the emotion in his voice. His hands were hot on her face. She wanted this to last.

Before she could manage another thought, she felt his lips close over hers. Her heart pounded in her ears. The soles of her feet warmed. This was not how she expected the day to end. She felt a pang of guilt for letting her thoughts wander from her dad, but Hedge pulled her legs across his lap and began kissing her neck and shoulders. She could barely breathe, let alone think.

"Is this all right?" he managed between kisses.

Evan pressed in and nodded. "You're the one who didn't want any fraternization, not me." Her fingers gripped his shoulders and pulled him closer.

Hedge's hands moved from her hips up her back. His fingers wove into her hair, lighting a fire wherever they touched. Evan felt her body melting into his when his phone began to vibrate and ring.

Both of them growled. Hedge helped her shift off his lap and then reached to answer. "It's Elle."

Evan started to roll her eyes and then realized that the call might be about her dad. She nodded and listened intently. Hedge pressed the speaker button.

"It's Hedge, you're on speaker."

Elle's voice sounded irritated. Evan knew she hated to be on speakerphone. "What do you know? Did you make contact with Calvin Moss?"

"Not exactly," Hedge began. He explained to her about finding him dead and about the man in the hat and the shooter, leaving out Evan's father's name. He told her that they'd done some digging on Moss and found out that he was going to meet someone called the Broker. He waited for her to volunteer any information.

Elle listened and made a clicking noise with her tongue. "The Broker? Are you certain of this?"

Evan leaned toward the phone. "Yes, do you know something about this man?"

Eleanor seemed to be hesitating. Evan wondered if she wanted Hedge to take it off speaker and have a private conversation. "Something came across my desk this morning. Intel says it may link to Michael Cooper. There's chatter about a couple of his companies being looked at by a broker. Some question as to who takes over now that he's deceased. They were calling in the broker. That's the word they used. It could be a coincidence. I didn't think twice about it until you used the term."

"Do we know who 'they' are? Where are we getting this intel?" Hedge nodded to Evan.

Elle hummed as if she was looking for the answer. "No particular source ID, but they note a meeting, or something, going down soon in Kyiv."

Evan shook her head. "I don't believe in too many coincidences."

"Me neither," Hedge added. "Do you want us in Kyiv? Do we have a date for this mystery meeting?"

They could hear Elle tapping at a keyboard. "Get some sleep tonight. I'll have your packets waiting for you at the front desk by the time you wake up."

"Roger that," Hedge said and clicked off. He tossed the phone back on the table and eyed Evan. "I know we kind of started something here, but—"

"But sunrise is in three and a half hours, and we have a big day tomorrow." Evan finished the thought. She leaned up and kissed his forehead. "We're good."

Hedge smiled as she walked to the bedroom. "You go on. I'll be in soon. Gonna shut everything down and get the lights."

Evan took a quick shower and dressed for bed, lingering as she brushed her teeth and hair. She almost hoped that Hedge had changed his mind and she would find him in her bed. But when she came out of the bathroom, the lights were still on and the bed was empty. She peeked back into the living room and found him asleep on the couch in the dark.

"G'night, Hedge," she whispered.

CHAPTER SEVEN

"I thought I had 24 hours before I was expected at a desk," Rowan Kirk moaned into his phone as he climbed the steps to the nondescript concrete building that housed the InDIGO offices in DC. "I'm still a little laggy."

"Then we're a matching set," Eleanor McKinnon-Grey chirped through the speaker. "Are you close? We can't delay."

"I'm at the front door." Kirk pushed through the thick glass double door and nodded to the short security guard waving him toward her.

"Good, I've told Salma to get you through check-in without all the fuss. I'll meet you up here." Elle clicked off without a goodbye.

Kirk dropped his phone into his shirt pocket as Salma did metal-detector-wand aerobics around his body. "Good morning, Salma."

"Yessir. Miss Eleanor says you better get up there quick. It's a mess. She's afraid heads will roll with this one." Salma pushed the green button on the side of her arch and practically pushed Kirk through toward the stainless-steel elevator doors. "Get on with yourself."

Kirk raised his brows. "Heads? What happened?" He could feel a warm flush climb up to his jet-lagged brain, pumping an extra shot of adrenaline into his system. He looked to Salma for an answer.

"Oh, no, sir. Not my story to tell. Miss Eleanor will get you squared. I don't want my pretty head rolling with the others. No, sir." She flipped the back of her hand his direction, dismissing him. Kirk could hear her muttering more as she turned back to her station, but couldn't make it out.

He stood in the elevator car, facing front and center, knowing Elle would drag him off as soon as the doors opened.

What could have happened in the last twelve hours? Evan was fine the last time he pinged her phone—roving the streets of Amsterdam. He hadn't heard from her yet this morning, but she knew he was taking a quick breather before going back to the office. And with her, no news was good news.

Ding. He was home.

He expected a slim, bangled wrist to grab his arm before the doors were all the way opened, but the hall was empty. He stepped out and looked both directions. Nobody. Not even at the little reception desk. He tucked his attache under his left arm and started to his right. The glass walls of offices flanking both sides of the corridor were all curtained as if the place were closed for a holiday. Except InDIGO didn't close for any holiday.

At the end of the hall, the space opened up to a large room with a centered pinwheel of desks that served as secretarial stations. Empty. He looked to the other side of the room where his old office had been located. Standing in the doorway was Elle, tethered by a corded phone, and waving her arms wildly in his direction.

"Get over here now," she yelled through a whisper.

Kirk picked up his walking pace as he circuited the desks. "What is going on? Where is everyone?"

Elle pointed to a new leather chair behind the glass-topped desk, and Kirk took a seat.

"I'm working on that right now, Max." Elle rolled her eyes. "Kirk is here, I'll call you back with a sit-rep in ten." She smashed the phone into the cradle and released a frustrated gasp. "That's the only good thing about a landline. You can't slam a cell phone without costing yourself a small fortune."

Kirk slid his new business laptop onto his desk and opened it, trying to remain calm. "What is going on? The place is empty, you're in full-on panic mode, and Salma's scared to talk. That's the real tell right there. Salma always talks."

Elle leaned over his desk and narrowed her glare toward Kirk. He'd never seen her like this.

"Shelby Templeton was found hanged in his cell last night.

Xandra Yakovsky has escaped."

Kirk swallowed and then exhaled. "But the security in this building is state-of-the-art with triple redundancies."

"I know." Elle pulled a wooden chair from the corner and plopped into it. "Not only that but internal, high clearance codes were used. She walked out without any cameras, without physical scans, without detection at all."

"That's impossible. You don't even have that kind of clearance." Kirk raked his fingers through his short crop of snow-white hair, as though it would help stimulate his brain. He took a few seconds to process the information. Templeton had been Anton Hrevic's party organizer. It was Evan's arrest of him that had started the whole mission. And Xandra was Anton's top model, or rather, Anton was Xandra's top puppet. If Xandra was out, Evan was in danger. "Did Xandra kill Templeton? Is that what we're thinking?"

Elle shrugged. "No cameras there, either. No evidence." She sighed and stood again. "Everyone who has been here—at this building—within the last 48 hours is in quarantine. They're all under the impression that we've had an anthrax scare. Nobody in or out. Phones running through Level Six Diagnostics." She smoothed her skirt over her hips. "I've already called Stan to let him know I won't be home for a couple more days." She tilted her head toward Kirk. "Do you have anyone you need to call?"

He knew she was referring to Delia, the woman he walked away from a decade ago when he was recruited into InDIGO. While he had recently been working on rekindling that relationship through email and social networking, they had no plans to meet yet. "The only person I need to get hold of is Evan. Xandra would like nothing better than to see her suffer."

Elle nodded and drew a deep breath. Kirk knew that was bad.

She began. "I agree with your assessment, however," she said with a pause, "Max wants all communication with field agents terminated immediately and until the method of breach can be determined and dealt with."

Kirk shook his head. "No. Absolutely not. This is Evan we're talking about. Xandra's escape directly affects her. And Hedge, too, remember?"

Elle placed her hands on her hips, though Kirk could tell it was for looks, and nothing more. She had to play the part of superior officer, but she was in the same boat he was. They both had personal connections with Evan and Hedge. "I know how you feel. But at this point, until we know how she got out, and who helped her, we can't risk it. We could be putting them in more danger."

"More danger than them roaming Europe blind?" Kirk pushed his chair back from his desk, wanting to grab his gear and go. "This is total crap, and you know it."

Elle looked as though Kirk had slapped her face with a cold fish. The word sprang from his lips before he could stop it. Kirk did not swear. Period. For him, even the word *crap* was an indicator that his world was crumbling around him. For him to use it with her, revealed more than he cared to. That he'd actually said the word *to her* surprised him as much as it shocked her.

He huffed to himself as his computer powered up, hoping to deflect her expression of astonishment. "And what are we—what am I supposed to do now? She's my partner."

"She's Hedge's partner." Elle softened her tone. "He will take care of her."

Kirk pounded a few keys to bring up the appropriate programs. "So I just sit here at this ridiculous desk going through data until I figure out who hacked our system?"

"You're the only one I trust to do it." Elle walked to the glass door, gesturing to a small refrigerator in the built-in credenza behind him. "You have water and sodas in there. I stashed a bottle of Patron in the bottom right-hand drawer. There's a lime in the fridge, too."

Kirk knew she didn't want to discuss their options any longer. She was under orders, and now he was, too. They could easily talk until they had justified whatever they really wanted to do. And the results would most likely get them demoted, fired, incarcerated, or worse. They had an understanding, anyway. Officially they would end their conversation. Unofficially, they could pursue off-book actions. Well, that was his understanding. He hoped it was hers.

She glanced down at the skinny gold watch on her wrist. "We have another shift coming up in 45 minutes. Can I bring you some breakfast? I'm about to order from the café downstairs."

He didn't miss a beat. "I want an inch-thick Belgian waffle with raspberry jam and confectioner's sugar. A poached egg on a separate plate. And a thermos of black coffee. French roast."

Elle nodded with a smile. "I take it that you agree not to contact Evan or Hedge until we figure this all out. Right?"

Kirk smiled back at her and laced his fingers together. He mentally reviewed all the proper responses and options as he flipped his palms outward and cracked his knuckles. "Yes, ma'am." He waited until she walked out of earshot. "As far as you know."

CHAPTER EIGHT

Evan and Hedge picked up their packet as they checked out of the INK hotel. Evan tucked the envelope into her bag as Hedge thanked the clerk and assured him that they would return soon. Evan hoped it was true. They'd shared a moment, however brief, and she wanted more. Hedge nodded to her without making eye-contact and then gestured to the street door. He was playing cool, as if last night had never happened. Considering what was coming, maybe that was best for now.

On the plane to Kyiv, the couple shuffled through the barebones file sent from Elle. Hedge shook his head. "I tried to let her know we were en route to Ukraine, but only got her voicemail."

"That's all I got with Kirk, too." Evan drew a deep breath. She made all the reasonable excuses. "They're probably in a meeting. You know how it is in office." She watched as Hedge shot her a frustrated frown, followed with a dubious nod. She added. "Most likely doing paperwork. If we're lucky, they'll have most of it done before we get back."

Evan slid a file page toward Hedge without looking at it. She left her hand in the middle of the page, like a paperweight holding the file in place on the tray table. She wanted Hedge to take her hand in his. Just a touch. Something.

As if he hadn't noticed, Hedge slipped the page from beneath her fingers and scanned it. "Hotel confirmation. C'mon, Elle, throw us a bone. This can't be all you have."

Evan pulled her hand back. Her daddy had always said that worrying about tomorrow never solved a problem—only wasted today. *Daddy, why did you have to put me in a position of worrying about you?* She'd been trying not to worry, but Hedge was obviously concerned, too, and maybe about much more than her dad.

The short flight to Kyiv was almost over, and Hedge

started stuffing the papers back into the envelope. Evan waited for him to get everything inside and secured, and then she took the file and dropped it back into her bag. After she pushed the tote under the seat in front of her, she carefully raised both tray tables and noticed Hedge's foot tapping against the side rail of the seat.

She shook her head. She wasn't going to wait for his cue. Evan took his hand and squeezed. "If we don't hear anything from them, that's probably good. We have our lead. The meeting. Maybe that's all we need for now. They know we can handle it on our own." Finally, Hedge squeezed her hand back. "I mean, the good news is that Elle doesn't know that my daddy is the broker. She'd have for sure pulled the plug on us if she was aware of that little tidbit."

Hedge chuffed and nearly smiled. "I suppose that's true."

"O'course it is." Evan leaned close to his face and smiled her widest grin. "Right now, the two of us know quite a bit more than Elle or Kirk. And I think it's safe to say that if they knew what we know, we'd be in a lot of trouble. So maybe it's good that we can't get in touch with them." She stared into the dark blue storm of his eyes. She could easily get lost in there. She wanted to.

He blinked, and she snapped back. She struggled to remember what she was saying and if she had made her point.

"I'm just concerned for you." Hedge's voice was little more than a whisper. "This could get bad, and I don't want you hurt."

Evan swallowed hard. She heard the stuck-in-his-throat emotion in his rasp. She leaned back in her seat and closed her eyes. "Hurt more than watching a partner get murdered, unable to stop it?"

"Yes." His whisper grew more gravelly. "I know it's hard to imagine. But there are things much worse than that." He held her hand tighter. "You may be forced to make choices."

That was it. The shadow that had been lurking in the back of her brain since she saw her daddy's face on that video. Evan couldn't imagine her father was capable of murder. But she'd seen it with her own eyes. He was part of her mission now. And not just on the fringe. Not a little side-step that can be left off the final report. He was neck-deep in it. And worse, she had no idea where he was or whose side he was on. Worry was an understatement.

Evan nodded. She felt a tear roll over her cheek before she realized she was crying. She reached up to wipe it away, but Hedge beat her to it. His hand cupped her jaw, and he leaned closer. "Whatever you need. Just ask. I'm your partner."

"And my senior officer." The thought just struck her. "Can I ask a favor?"

"Anything."

She opened her eyes and found herself inches away from Hedge's face. She didn't want to ask. She didn't want to talk at all. But she had to. "If you're ordered… if you are told to do something to my daddy," she said, her voice choking.

"Stop. Don't go there." He sat back but kept his gaze steady.

Evan shook her head. "But isn't that what you meant?"

Hedge closed his eyes for a second, and Evan watched his chest rise and fall as he regrouped. "I don't want you to worry about that. I'm your partner. Yours."

"But if Elle or Fischer orders you?"

"Yours."

Evan felt her throat tightening. He was telling her that he would defy direct orders for her. That he would sacrifice himself for her. The words were sweet on his tongue, but they crackled and hissed, bitter in her ears.

"Can you hear me?"

Evan nodded. "I hear you."

Hedge wrinkled his brow. "What?"

"I hear you. I understand." She inhaled, wishing their circumstances were different.

"Not Hedge, Evan. It's me. Can you hear me?" Evan startled at the sound of Kirk's voice in her ear. She jumped enough that the lap belt snugged her to the seat.

She gestured to her left ear. "Red," she whispered. "We've

been trying to reach you."

Hedge leaned in, though he couldn't hear anything.

"I know," Kirk said. "I only have a second. I'm not supposed to contact you. Nobody is."

"Why? What's goin' on?"

"Xandra's out. Don't know how, yet. You two watch each other's backs. You're on your own for a bit. I'll shout if I can, but for now, you need to go dark." Another crackle in her ear.

"Wait, Red. What do you mean?" Evan was desperate for more. But there was no more.

Hedge shrugged. "What was that?"

Evan didn't know what to say or how. "It was Kirk. He said we're on our own for now. And then he was just gone."

"What does he mean? What happened?" Hedge lowered his voice, but his tone intensified. "What else did he say?"

The flight attendant tapped Hedge's shoulder and said something in Dutch. Evan assumed she was asking him to adjust the seat for landing. He nodded, inclined his seat, and smiled as she proceeded down the center aisle.

Evan pressed her lips together into a thin line, collecting her thoughts. She turned to face Hedge, taking his hand. "Kirk says that Xandra is out."

She looked out the window at the sprawling metropolis below them. Three million people, with a pretty good chance that at least a couple of them wanted her dead.

CHAPTER NINE

Hedge shifted the pale green drapes of their hotel room to peek at the parking lot below. More foot traffic than cars. The hotel was located near the secondary airport for Kyiv, and most guests took shuttles into the city's center. He went back to dressing while Evan got ready in the adjacent bathroom.

The room was small, stark, and clean, with no frills to speak of, by American standards. The furniture included two narrow twin beds on either side of a small nightstand. A single, round mirror was centered above. On the opposite wall stood a slim armoire beside a table-desk combo. The chair at the desk was the only piece of furniture in the room not permanently affixed in place. Everything but the chair was wood-grained plastic laminate over particle board. All the bed and bath linens were white.

There was no artwork on the walls. An air-conditioner, mounted high on the wall over the desk, blew relatively cool air toward the beds.

Hedge stood over the nightstand, straightening his tie in the mirror. "We'll take public transportation for most of the day. There will still be a lot of walking."

Evan finished her makeup in the slightly larger mirror over the wall mounted bathroom sink. "And I won't look conspicuous on a subway in a cocktail dress at," she checked the time on her phone, "eight forty-five in the morning?"

Hedge shook his head, though he knew Evan couldn't see him. "No. Not in Ukraine. Have you never been this far east before?"

Evan stepped through the bathroom door, and Hedge instantly felt the temperature in the room rise. Her eyes sparkled. "I am—or was—a fashion model. I did Paris, London, Milan, Hong Kong, and Tokyo." She paused, and Hedge could almost feel her teal blue gaze roam over his gray suit. "Ukraine was never on my itinerary."

He returned the favor, starting with her candy-red heels, grazing his way over her slim ankles, curvy calves, to her perfectly shaped body under the little black dress. He lingered a moment to imagine the henna butterfly on her back. Her hands rested at her trim waist, forming an artistic, almost architectural line to her bare shoulders. Evan's red curls were piled up on her head in a Greek goddess-style.

"Perfect," he said without thinking.

"Oh, no. None of that *perfect* talk. We already had that conversation."

Hedge dipped his chin in acknowledgment. "Yes. You're right. Not perfection, but definitely something close." He waggled his finger as was his routine to request an inspection spin. He'd always checked the dress before he and Evan went out, but today he was particularly thorough. The dress looked great. Evan was stunning. But something was biting at his mind. The only other woman to wear the dress was Xandra Yakovsky. She had knocked out Evan, stripped it from her unconscious body, tried to steal the technology and then murder her.

Evan had fought hard to get the dress back. She saved the mission, not to mention his life. But Xandra was in the wind again, and Hedge was scared. On a good day, Xandra was mean. She hated Evan. And with her resources, Xandra could be anywhere in the world.

"Is the dress ready?" Evan's voice rattled him back.

Hedge pulled on his jacket and holstered his weapon beneath it. He patted the laptop on the desk. "I have it set to signal us both if anyone matching Xandra or Costa pings the face-rec program."

Evan drew a deep breath. "Or anyone else from the primary case files? Right?"

"Right." Hedge handed Evan her purse from where it lay on her bed. "And you haven't heard anything from your dad or from Kirk?"

Evan raised her perfectly shaped brows. "I would tell you if I did."

Hedge offered his elbow to her as they reached the bedroom door. "And I would tell you." He turned to make sure the door had locked automatically. "We're all set."

"And what are we doing now? Just walking around Kyiv hoping to run into our target at the supermarket?" Evan's voice sounded skeptical.

"No. We have an address. Cooper has met with someone here a few times. Could be Costa, but we need to make sure. And if someone is here to meet the Broker, assuming your dad is THE Broker, we need to figure this out before he gets hurt." Hedge lowered his voice as another couple entered the hallway and walked just ahead of them to the elevator.

Hedge felt Evan's tug at his elbow. He stopped and sighed loudly. "I forgot the keys."

Evan held her purse between them and opened the kiss lock. "Let me see if I have them."

They poked through the spartan contents of her purse while the strangers got into the elevator and let the door close. They waited for the gears to whir before returning to their conversation.

Evan tightened her grip on his arm as the elevator car returned. He liked that she was prepared for anything. The lift was empty, and they got in.

Hedge stared at the floor numbers as they descended. To his disappointment, the doors didn't open until they reached ground level. Another passenger would have been cause for playful banter or even a lustful kiss. Instead, they merely stared at each other in anticipation of a busy day.

"You know your way around this place?" Evan asked as they walked toward the airport shuttle station.

"I do. I spent a week here once, during the last war. Everything was a mess. People moving from the battle zone to Kyiv, or as far west as they could get, as quickly as possible. Remind me, and one day I'll show you a photo of my friend and I standing in front of an unexploded mortar that landed in the middle of the road about twenty seconds before we got there."

"And so you took a selfie with it?" Evan rolled her eyes.

"No. Pasha and I took turns taking each others' pictures. Not technically a selfie." Hedge gestured toward a concrete column with the number six painted on the side. "This one."

Evan nodded and joined the small crowd gathering under the six as Hedge went to pay an elderly man at the counter.

"Was she pretty?" Evan asked as Hedge returned.

"Who?"

"Pasha. I imagine a gorgeous brunette with high cheekbones and dark brown eyes." Evan's eyes flashed as she slipped her hand back into the crook of Hedge's elbow.

Hedge laughed. "Pasha was blond, actually. On the chubby side and short." He waited for Evan to frown at his description. "And his beard was kind of bushy."

"I thought Pasha was a woman's name." Evan leaned heavy on Hedge's arm. "I was almost jealous."

Hedge clicked his tongue. "I knew you would. That's why I called him Pasha instead of Pavel. But don't be jealous of him. He's taking the big sleep now."

Evan glanced over her shoulder, making sure nobody was listening to them. "Did you make that happen for him?"

Hedge frowned. "No. My job was to deliver him from Donetsk to Kyiv, which I did. No. He did himself in. Vodka and cigarettes and a few other vices. Most men don't make sixty in this country. He was a week shy of sixty-two when I got word he was gone."

"That's a shame."

"Hardly. He was a fun guy to be around. That was true. But he'd killed a couple dozen people by the time he was thirty and had lost count by the time I'd met him. Garrot for hire, so to speak. Anyone for money, but he specialized in young female embassy workers. He would make a little on the side selling IDs he'd stolen from them."

"Nasty." Evan shook her head.

"Very." Hedge placed his hand over hers and led her to the front of the line as the shuttle approached. He whispered. "Get on and sit down. Keep your purse secure. Don't smile at anyone, even me."

"But I'm a Texan, smilin' is what we do." Evan started to break out into a smile, but Hedge raised his finger as a warning.

"I'm serious. If you smile, you'll inform everyone here that you're American. Translation: easy." Hedge lowered his voice further. "Even if you're not." He watched Evan's lips twitch and struggle against a grin.

They rode the bus into town, past dilapidating apartments and businesses, through parks punctuated with busts, sculpture, and monument plaques, to another bus station. Hedge stood and led them off the bus and onto the street. He muttered as he passed the driver. "D'akuju."

The man didn't respond, which didn't surprise Hedge. He looked around the stop, scanning faces for a minute, and then placed his hand in the center of Evan's back. "Over there." He pointed to another building at the far end of the block from them. "You're about to ride on the deepest metro in the world."

As they walked, Evan's grip grew tighter. Hedge decided not to let on that subways made him nervous, or that this one had almost triggered a panic attack the first time he rode it. It wasn't the depth of the train, or even the fact that the cars hadn't seen maintenance since the late seventies. It was the crowds. Too many people pressing too close. He wasn't claustrophobic, but he didn't like situations that could go wildly out of control without warning. The subway—this subway—was the epitome of chaos at the best of times.

They went through the street doors and through the turnstiles with a few hundred others heading to work. Then came the escalators. Hedge swallowed hard at the first step down. Evan stood in front of him but then immediately turned to face him. "I can't even see the bottom of this thing."

Hedge almost let himself smile at her reaction. "I know. And there is another set of escalators after this."

Evan stood on her toes, blocking his view of the people directly in front of them. The tunnel down to the train platforms was lit only with the lamps that protruded from the center dividers of the slow-moving staircases. The globes over the lights were printed with warnings not to slide down the divisions.

They stepped from the first set of stairs, across a stretch of concrete and onto another escalator exactly like the first. Evan's jaw dropped. Hedge pressed his lips together to remind her not to gawk. She raised her fingers to her lips and whispered. "This is crazy. I feel like we could get the bends if we went back up too fast."

Hedge realized that he heard her without actually seeing her speak. The earwigs were working.

They found their desired platform and waited for the subway to arrive. Hedge murmured, "When the doors open, get on. Do not let go of my hand. Do not worry about your manners. Your mother isn't here. I will drag or push you if I have to. Is that clear?"

"Yessir."

The train whooshed into place and stopped with a screech and a clunk. The doors slid open, and a wall of people spilled out. As he expected, Evan paused to let others go in front of her. Hedge wrapped his arm around her waist and pulled her onto the car as the doors slipped shut behind them.

"That wasn't even enough time to know if this is the right train." Evan turned into Hedge's arms, clutching her purse between them.

Hedge tilted his head with a sympathetic smirk. "Honey, it was enough time for eighty-five people to get on in front of you."

Evan tipped her head back and looked into Hedge's eyes. He could see a hint of nerves bubbling just below the surface. He didn't want her to see his.

"How much of this day will be spent on the metro?" Her voice trembled.

"We'll take this one to Independence Square and then the one back. I think we can walk everything else." He relaxed a bit when he saw a hint of relief flash over her face. "And I know where we can get a good cup of borscht."

"I'm not eatin' borscht."

"It's delicious. You are eating it." Hedge kept a firm hold of Evan's waist until after they were off the metro and back up in the sunlight. He started to turn loose, but she reached around his waist to walk side-by-side.

"Do you have the address?" Evan asked. Her head swiveled back and forth as they walked into Maidan Square. The center parkway was dotted with fountains and glass domes that funneled light into the underground shops. Tall brick and granite buildings lined the square on either side.

Hedge directed her toward the far end of the oblong park. "It should be down there, on one of the spoke streets behind the McDonald's."

"You're kidding, right?" Evan scanned the buildings ahead and found the bright yellow arches. "You're not kidding."

Hedge frowned. "No. And before you ask, *no*, we're not eating at McDonald's."

They walked for another ten minutes before reaching the franchise. They shifted their arms from around the other's waists to a simple hand-hold once they started down the side street, and the crowds diminished dramatically.

The sun was almost directly overhead, making the stone veneers of the buildings seem darker than they really were. Hedge scanned for addresses. They still had another block or two to go. "Did you notice," he began. His sudden conversation seemed to startle Evan. "Sorry. But we didn't get a single notification from the dress surveillance."

"I wasn't going to say anything and jinx it." Evan smiled.

He hadn't realized how much he missed seeing her nearly-constant grin until she banished it for their city excursion. He smiled back. "I don't think you can jinx something like that."

"The address is just up here." Hedge motioned toward a rust-colored building with cut stone pediments over the doors and windows. Several pockmarks showed in the brick all the way down the walls. "See these? Bullet holes." He took a deep breath, remembering.

"And did you put them here?" Evan asked with a wink.

"Not these." Hedge chuffed. "At least not all of them."

Evan cocked her head and frowned. "Now, don't tell stories to impress me. I know if you're lying."

Hedge nodded. "Yes, you do. Can you hear any ticking?" He waited as she listened for the dress to tick in her ear receiver as it did when it detected deception.

Evan furrowed her brow. "Did you really get into a gunfight right here?"

Hedge shrugged. "Not just here. We were fighting all over this place. A couple streets over is where Pasha saved my life." He laughed and then stopped short. "That's the place we're looking for."

He pulled Evan to his side and leaned against the building across the street from their target. "Andriy Popovic, Photographer. Weddings."

Evan twisted her lips to one side. "That can't be right."

Hedge shrugged again. "It's the right address."

"Do we go in?"

Hedge shook his head. "No. Let's watch for a minute and see who goes in and who comes out."

Evan nodded. She pulled out her phone to check for missed calls or messages. Hedge did the same.

They turned at the sound of a bell and saw a young couple exiting the photo studio. Just a bride and groom making big plans. Hedge dipped his chin as they passed.

They waited again. Hedge turned to watch them walk all the way to the corner and disappear into the main square.

"What's wrong?" Evan asked.

"I feel like we're missing something."

Evan reached out for his hand. "Missing something? What do you mean?"

Hedge scratched at his chin. He was letting his goatee grow back in, and his whiskers were starting to itch. "I don't know. It's like we've forgotten something."

Evan poked at his arm. "We did. Him."

"Who?" Hedge asked as a man in a hat stepped out of the studio. Both he and Evan turned to look inside the storefront window when they saw the man walking their direction. Hedge realized it was the same man who had been with Evan's father in the video of Calvin Moss's murder. The man in the hat passed behind them without glancing their way.

"Do we follow him or do we go into the shop and make sure he hasn't left anyone dead inside?" Evan looked over her shoulder toward the shop and then toward the man.

Hedge did the same, and as soon as he made eye contact with the man, the man ran. "Question answered."

Evan nodded and immediately took to chase. Hedge followed, impressed with how fast she could run in heels. He had almost caught up with her when hat-man vanished into a doorway beneath a red and gold canopy. They both stopped and studied the entrance before proceeding.

"It's an Indian restaurant." Hedge kept Evan behind him. "Just opened for lunch. We go inside. I'll go right, you left. Do you have your weapon ready?"

Evan held up her purse with one hand inside. "I really don't want to blow a hole in this bag."

Hedge unholstered his pistol, keeping it tucked just inside his jacket. "Better the purse than somewhere else."

Hedge went in first, walking through the dark foyer into a small dining room appointed with red-stained wooden everything. Gold curtains swagged either side of an alcove on the opposite wall. Evan had moved to the left side of the room, bumping open a double-swing door to the kitchen, and sweeping it quickly. Hedge rounded the right side of the room, hurrying to the alcove. He pushed back one drape, and then the other. The place was empty. "Anything?" he whispered.

Evan answered in his earwig. "Two cooks and the owner. All women. You?"

Hedge shook his head as they met at the back. "No one.

And I didn't see a back door. How did this guy get out?"

Evan nudged his left arm. "Did you check behind there?"

Hedge looked to his left and saw a curtain pulled in front of a hallway marked *WC*. "The restroom." He paced toward the hall, gesturing for Evan to stay behind him. "I'll check the toilets, you keep watch on the door."

Scanning the hall, Hedge pushed the sheer drape back and stepped toward the door to the right.

"Shcho ty tut robysh?" a woman from the kitchen shouted.

Hedge turned to explain that he was looking for a man, but before he could utter a word, hat-man bolted from behind the opposite door, crashing into him and knocking both Hedge and Evan against a table. He ran for the door with the couple a dozen steps behind.

As they pushed through the street door, sunlight blinded Hedge for a second. His eyes adjusted slowly, and he saw the man at the corner. He wasn't running.

"Down!" Evan yelled, but her voice was interrupted by a loud pop. Evan smashed into Hedge, sending him all the way down this time. He looked back to the corner. The man was gone.

He pulled himself to sitting and reached over to Evan. She didn't move. Blood oozed from the corner of her mouth. She'd been shot.

He scooped her up into his lap, and she moaned. She was alive.

"Are you alright?" he asked. "Where are you hit?"

Evan pushed at his shoulder. "I'm fine. Go get him."

"I'm not leaving you. You've been shot." He held her to his chest. "Stay with me."

"You big idiot. I'm okay. I think he might have bruised a rib, but this dress is bullet-proof. Go find him." Evan sat up and clutched at her side. "Ow. It hurts like a hell-hound, but I'm not dying."

"What?" Hedge looked over her body, checking for wounds. He rubbed the smear of blood from her lips with his thumb. "You're okay?"

Evan grimaced as she pulled herself to her feet, still holding her side. "You let him get away." She yanked off her right shoe and shook a rock out. Stepping back into it and shaking her head, she said, "Why didn't you go after him when I told you?"

"I thought you were hurt." Hedge climbed back to his feet. "I'm not leaving you to die somewhere alone."

"Whether I'm alone or with you doesn't matter if I'm dead. This is the job. You know that as well as I do. Better, even." Evan growled. Hedge knew she was hurting. He reached out for her hand, but she batted it away. "Do you know the grief I'm gonna catch from Kirk and Elle about this?"

Hedge couldn't listen to any more of this. He took her into his arms as gently as he could and kissed her blood-tinged mouth. "Listen," he whispered as their lips parted. "Don't ever ask me to leave you again." He took a step away from her. A thousand realizations hit him at the same time, and he wasn't sure what to do with any of them. This was going to be more complicated than he imagined.

Still in a daze, Evan sighed and grasped his arm again. "Do I still have to eat borscht?"

Hedge shook his head and forced a smile. "No. Is the dress back online?" He waited for Evan to check for the signal in her ear.

Evan paused for a moment and then nodded.

"Good. Let's go on back now and see if we can pull an ID this time. Surely the dress cameras caught his face today."

Evan squeezed his arm tightly as they stepped back into the crowded parkway. Hedge scanned every face they passed, afraid that the dress would ping on one before they could get back to their hotel. Evan must have felt the same urgency. Even in pain, she kept a quick pace with him all the way to the metro station. Hedge positioned his body on her injured right side, protecting her from any accidental bumps in the crowd.

Another realization slammed into his brain. She had saved his life. Again.

CHAPTER TEN

Every inch of Evan's body throbbed in pain. She had never been shot before, and the impact shook her to the bone.

The Little Black Dress had worked precisely as designed. The microsensors woven throughout the fabric detected the projectile and released a sonic-electromagnetic pulse in response. The SEM pulse caused a ripple in the air which disrupted the trajectory of the bullet, causing a slight turn and slowing down the projectile considerably. The laminated fabric of the dress and the armored corset prevented penetration.

It still hurt.

Evan pushed through the pain to keep up with Hedge's yard-long strides as they hurried from Independence Square to the metro. She wasn't thrilled to go back into the depths and crowds of the subway terminal, but it would get her closer to the cover of their hotel room. And relative safety.

Down the escalator, she scanned the faces of everyone around her. She had no trouble not smiling at them now. Hedge kept her tucked against his side as they found the right platform. She felt his steady grip around her body as he practically lifted her over the yellow line and into the train car. The number of riders had only increased since their earlier trip. She was a sardine in a can, racing from one point to another at over 100 kilos an hour.

Once they got back to the street, Hedge gestured to the bus stop across the corner. "Do you need anything to eat before we board the bus?" His voice was soft in her ear, and she barely saw his lips move.

"No, let's keep going." She wasn't sure how loud she spoke. Her ears thumped with her pulse and the lingering screech of the metro.

He acknowledged with a dip of his chin and led her onto the bus. They found a seat on the row in front of the back side door, and Evan slid to window side. She closed her eyes as the trip back began.

They both sat in silence. Evan became hypersensitive to everything around her. The itchy fabric of the seat. The rumble of the bus's drivetrain rattling up through the floor, through her shoes, to the soles of her feet. The compression of the corset against her bruised ribcage. The clamminess of her bare arms. Hedge's warm arm stretched across her shoulders. The wind blowing in through the window, buffeting her face.

Growing up in Texas, she had always held a grudge against the wind. It threw dust and sand everywhere and ruined whatever hairstyle she wore. It ruined picnics and photos. It made the cold colder and the heat hotter. But right now, she loved it.

Right now, with the warm air powdering her cheeks and lashes, she felt a calm sense of home. They had survived, and they would keep on surviving.

Then a young man from the row in front of them stood up and closed the window. He nodded slightly in her direction as if to say *you're welcome*. The wind was gone. The stale smell of decades-old perspiration permeated the air. She let her shoulders sink with her heart.

Hedge must have sensed her disappointment. "Look there. Three o'clock."

To her right, Evan saw they were passing a lush green park with a granite bust of some historical figure marking the entrance. In at least three vignettes around the park, brides and grooms posed for photos in front of flowers or archways.

"Is this national wedding picture day or something?" she asked.

"This happens all day, every day here." Hedge pointed to

another couple posing in front of old wood doors of a court-house or some sort of official building. As if to punctuate his statement, a long black convertible, bedecked with flowers and streamers, passed the bus with its horn blaring. A bride and groom waved from the back seat as other drivers honked and waved.

Evan started to laugh, but the split-second muscle con-traction sent a stabbing pain up to her brain and stars flashed in her eyes. "Ouch."

Hedge pulled her head gently against him and leaned his jaw against her forehead. "When we get back to the room, I'll give you a good once over and let the dress run diagnostics on you before we do anything else."

Evan drew a deep breath and released it slowly. The pain level stayed the same. Not good, but bearable. "I don't think any-thing is broken."

"We'll know for sure soon."

They traveled on through Kyiv, the bus occasionally stop-ping to drop off and pick up passengers. The bus passed the air-port and slowed to a stop. They were almost back. Only a short walk to the hotel.

Leaving the bus, they walked past a few more busses. Evan held tightly to Hedge's arm, chanting *almost there* over and over in her mind. They dodged a crowd of people disembarking from another bus. Stepping off the sidewalk to avoid the stragglers, Evan saw him. The man in the hat.

She squeezed Hedge's arm, but he had seen him too.

The man in the hat appeared shocked to see them both alive. Evan took a step behind Hedge as he drew his pistol. Their opponent glanced around him, obviously looking for cover. He had nowhere to run.

Hedge raised his weapon in his right hand and held out his left as a warning. "Don't move. Ne rukhaysya."

Panic showed on the man's face. Evan watched as the man tried to calculate his chances of defeating Hedge in a gunfight or outrunning him with only a few yards' headstart. He must have preferred his odds in a race because he immediately ran back into the crowds at the bus terminal.

"Don't shoot him," Evan reminded Hedge as he lowed his sidearm and took chase. "He can lead us to Costa or to my dad. We need him alive."

"I know." Hedge ran ahead and disappeared into the crowd too. Evan followed but didn't run. She managed a quick pace that didn't jostle too much. They were close. This time they would catch him and make him talk. He had been with her dad in Amsterdam. Whose side was he on? Whose side was her dad on? He would talk. She would make him talk.

As Evan hurried through the mass of people in lines for the next busses, she could hear the universal sound of murmurs and questions. Though she didn't understand Ukranian, she knew they wondered what was happening. Grown men don't chase each other unless something bad is happening.

A young woman in a gray uniform stepped out in front of her with her hands up in halt. She coughed out an order that Evan couldn't translate but definitely understood. She stopped and held her empty palms up and out.

The woman took another step toward her but stopped at the squeal of bus brakes and the loud thud of something being hit. Gasps and short screams came from a few yards ahead. Both women turned and ran to the sounds.

Evan had almost reached the scene when Hedge's strong arm reached out and pulled her aside. As dozens of people ran toward the front of a bus stopped in the middle of the road, Evan and Hedge walked the other direction.

"You don't need to see that." Hedge shook his head when Evan searched his face for an explanation.

They plodded back to the hotel and up to their room. Evan sank onto the foot of the bed next to the window, and Hedge took a seat in the chair and opened up the laptop. As soon as the program initiated, Evan heard a familiar voice in her ear. "You made it back to your room."

"Kirk!" she gasped. "Link with Hedge's earwig too. We've had a terrible morning."

Hedge nodded as he started the physical diagnostic program with the LBD. "I'm here, Kirk. What can you tell us?"

"You two are in danger." Kirk's tone was cool, but Evan detected more than a hint of worry.

"We know that." Hedge rolled his eyes.

Evan shook her head and interrupted. "Hey, Red. I got shot this morning. On the bright side, the dress worked perfectly. I'm still alive."

Kirk sounded as if he barely heard her. "You need to get out of your room and find a safe house. Like now."

Hedge took a deep breath. "We're working on it. I'm running the LBD bios on Evan to make sure she doesn't have any broken ribs."

Evan heard Kirk tapping on his program. "Okay, but you have less than ten minutes before you will be taken into custody by another InDIGO agent. I don't have any idea what is happening or why, but I intercepted a memo on something earlier. You are to be brought in. Mission over. Use of force approved if necessary."

"What are we supposed to do?" Evan's mind stretched to understand why the mission had been cut short. By whom?

"I don't know who authorized the memo. I don't know any details at all. Yesterday I was told not to—under any circumstances—contact you. Today it's like you're on the Most Wanted List. Make sure Evan is good, and then get out of there. Do you hear me?" Kirk's voice lost all semblance of calm. "I can't stay with you much longer. I'll contact you when it's safe."

Evan's head ached. Everything seemed blurry. "We can pack up our gear and be out in five minutes."

Kirk yelled this time. "You are not listening to me. Don't take anything with you. Ditch the dress. Get out of it now. Leave the laptop. Leave the dress, the shoes, everything. I'm sending you a photo of the agent who's on his way to you now. Avoid him. There are at least two more that are just a few minutes behind him. I don't have photos of them."

The computer dinged, and a picture popped up at the bottom of the screen. Hedge and Evan exchanged a confused glance.

"Are you sure this is an InDIGO agent coming for us?" Evan asked.

"Yes," Kirk said. "Did you get the picture?"

Evan stood and started undressing quickly. "We did." She kicked off her shoes and tossed them into the corner. "He's the man who shot me this morning."

Hedge peeled off his jacket and tie as he read the results from the diagnostics. "Evan has the all-clear. Nothing broken. No internal bleeding. We'll find a safe place as soon as possible."

Kirk's voice took a more urgent tone. "Listen, this guy is close. You need to move now."

"Kirk, we're okay." Evan carefully pulled on a pair of jeans and a black tee shirt. "That man is dead. We have an extra minute or two."

"You killed him? Hedge?" Kirk asked.

Hedge dumped his duffle bag onto his bed. "I was chasing him. He ran in front of a bus."

"Good. If I get photos of anyone else to watch for, I'll send them to your safe house—if you want me to know where you are. I'll leave that up to you. Don't trust anyone. Really, don't even trust me. Just stay safe. Don't try to contact me. I don't know how secure my regular channels are anymore." He didn't say good-bye. He was just gone.

Thoughts swirled in Evan's mind as she prepared to run. Protocol dictated that she take nothing that might contain a tracker, which was practically everything. She dumped her purse. Nothing she couldn't live without. Her suitcase. Again, nothing. She holstered her Springfield and put on another coat of lipstick. She would have to replace everything later.

She went into the bathroom and brushed through her hair. Couldn't take the brush. She stared at her hair in the mirror. Red hair, red flag. She returned to the bedroom to find Hedge was dressed in jeans and a tee also.

He must have been thinking the same thing she was because he tossed her Hermes scarf at her. "Wrap up your hair. How much time do you need?"

"I can be ready to go in three minutes." Evan pulled her hair into a low ponytail, twisted it into a bun, and then began wrapping it all with the scarf until only a few tendrils showed at her temples.

"Make it one." He handed her his navy blue dress shirt. "Put this on. It will help conceal your pistol."

Evan picked up her wallet after she had the shirt on. She could still smell his aftershave on the collar. She breathed in deep to enjoy the second. She realized the pain in her ribs was lessening. She smiled at Hedge. He was tucking his weapon into his waistband and looking for a shirt to put on over his tee.

"Do I take my billfold? We're gonna need some money."

"Take the cash. Leave everything else. I have a box with a burner and some money. We'll be fine."

Tucking the money into her bra, Evan shrugged. "I suppose I'm ready to go."

Hedge reached out for her hand. He looked over the room again as he opened the door. "Leaving the dress is harder than I expected."

Evan stepped into the hall and scanned floor to ceiling in both directions. "Clear."

Hedge tugged at her arm. "Wait. I need to leave the earwig." He tossed the small plastic receiver across the room before closing the door.

They hurried down the hall to the stairwell and started down the stairs to the first floor when Evan heard clicking in her ear. "Stop," she whispered to Hedge. She pointed to her ear.

Soft bumps and thuds sounded in her ear receiver. She couldn't make anything out until she heard a man's voice release a series of swears and curses in a thick Russian accent. "They're gone." The man paused for a moment. "I don't know. All of their things are here, but it's a mess." Another pause. "Wait." His voice was louder. "I have an earpiece. If it's connected, we can track it, maybe."

Evan quickly pulled her earrings out and tucked them into her jeans pocket. "Someone's in the room. A man, and he's talking to someone else. They're probably outside watching for us. I didn't recognize his voice, but he was Russian for sure."

Hedge looked down at her sneakers. "Can you run if you have to?"

Evan nodded and held up her hand, clasped in his. "Just don't let go."

CHAPTER ELEVEN

They made their way out of the hotel through a side door that faced the series of small service buildings between the hotel and the airport. Evan could see the police staged around the bus terminal at the street, still questioning a few witnesses. She noticed a few bystanders who could have been agents watching for them.

She followed Hedge into a garage area where they found a minivan with a shuttle service logo on the doors. "We have our ride back to town."

Within a few minutes, he had the keys from a numbered board on the wall. He slid the side door opened and helped her inside. "Sit in the back."

Evan grabbed a ball cap from the seat beside her and handed it up to Hedge. "Put this on. There might be cameras." She hadn't seen any so far, but they were about to pass the airport, which would be loaded with security.

They drove back toward the city's center without being noticed. She hoped.

At the south end of Independence Square, Hedge parked the van in front of a post office. The tall, cut-stone building sat on the corner with 40-foot tall arches guarding the massive wooden doors. "My box is in here. Do you want to wait here or come in with me?"

"Hmm... should I sit in a stolen minivan all alone or go with you?" She smirked. "Guess which I prefer."

"Then come on."

She took his arm and escorted him into the old building. Everything was pale gray marble or granite or plaster. The coffered ceiling was braced with polished marble columns. Evan felt as though she was walking into a palace instead of a post office.

Hedge removed the ball cap and nodded toward a security guard. She followed him as he confidently walked through a less-grand archway into a room lined with post boxes. A clerk sat at a desk and shot a bored look in their direction, but didn't offer to help.

Hedge pulled a small key from his pocket, opened the miniature metal door, and removed a plain brown cardboard box. He tucked it under his arm, and they went back to the van.

"I figured we were going to leave the car and walk from here." Evan scooted to the end of the bench seat to leave room for Hedge, with the box between them. "What's the plan?"

Hedge opened the box and emptied it into the space between them. Two passports, two ID cards, two credit cards, and a bundle of Ukrainian currency sat in a neat stack beside a spare magazine of ammunition for Hedge's pistol and a small black flip phone.

"I'll make a call to a friend. If he's still alive, he can turn these into official documents by midnight. He can probably find us a place to stay as well." Hedge looked pleased with himself.

"And no ties to InDIGO?"

"None whatsoever."

"What are we going to do about this car?" Evan eyed the street traffic. She was glad she didn't have to drive in it.

"We'll park it at the bus terminal over there." He gestured to a canopy on the next block. "No one will think twice about it. If we're lucky, the shuttle company will think one of their drivers just took it for a joy ride."

Hedge got back into the driver's seat, and five minutes later, they were walking the square again. They sat on a stone bench so that Hedge could make his call. He spoke quickly, switching from Ukrainian to Russian and back, which Evan assumed matched the other side of the conversation. They had taken care of all their business in ninety seconds, and when Hedge snapped the phone closed, he patted her hand. "Everything's going to be fine."

"Can we get something to eat? I'm kind of starving," Evan said. "My stomach growled at least three times during your conversation. At this point, I would even eat borscht."

"Good, because that's where Dima is meeting us." Hedge pointed to a green canopy-topped door on the far end of the building behind them. "You'll like it."

Evan rolled her eyes. She was sure she would hate it, but when they walked into the dark little cafeteria-style restaurant, she inhaled the luxurious aroma of seasoned chicken and roasted vegetables. Her stomach growled loudly enough for Hedge to hear it.

"Let's get you fed." He led her through the line, ordering for her and carrying the tray of food to a candle-lit corner table. "You really will like it."

Evan wanted to argue, but the large bowl of soup seduced her into trying a spoonful. And then another. Tomatoes and carrots and chicken bathed in broth and herbs and danced with all sorts of spices she couldn't identify. She couldn't decide if she was just starving, or if this was the best bowl of stew she'd ever eaten. Maybe she was still in shock.

"She is too beautiful for you, old man," a voice sounded from behind her.

Hedge laughed. "You're right about that, friend."

A stout man in his mid-forties took a seat at their table. He hooked a small satchel over the back of Evan's chair. "I have all your paperwork in there. It is finished. You just give me the old forms. I can make good use of them."

Evan frowned. "How can you have all the details right? You don't have photos. You haven't had time."

Hedge chuffed. "She makes a good point, Dima. You were never so fast before."

The man laced his fingers over his chest. "Hedge, you hurt me. The woman I can forgive. She doesn't know me, but you do."

"Perhaps that's why I doubt."

Dima shrugged. "Take a look if you like. I have internet now. I have better equipment. Amazon can get you anything."

Hedge picked up the satchel and opened it. He handed a passport and ID card to Evan. She inspected them carefully. They looked perfect. The passport even had real stamps from around the globe. The photos were from the last fashion show she had done in Milan.

"Incredible." Evan smiled at Dima.

"Impeccable. Really, Dima, you've outdone yourself." Hedge slid the old documents from his post box to his friend. "And what else do I owe you?"

"Nothing at all. We're square, as you say." Dima patted the bag. "You can keep the handbag, too. If you like it." He sighed. "And as a bonus, your IDs are all backstopped online. They're clean. No flags at any borders. My daughter has a gift for photoshop. Even if they run your scanned photos through Facial Recognition, it won't hit."

"Your daughter? Little Susha?" Hedge held out his hand as if he measured a meter up from the ground.

"She is grown now. Ready to take over the family business. Just waiting for me to die." He laughed and winked at Evan. "You know how she feels?"

Evan frowned at the idea and then heard a bump under the table. Dima gasped and reached for his leg.

"I'm sorry. I should keep my mouth shut." Dima stood.

"Forgive me, dear."

"It's nothing." Evan pasted her smile back on, but now it was less sincere.

Dima bowed at the waist and stretched out his hand to Hedge. "I almost forgot. Give me your phone." Hedge handed him the flip phone, and Dima gave him a blister pack of two burner phones with a separate package containing SIM cards. He took a card from his jacket pocket and slipped it into Evan's hand. "This address is empty for the next month. The pantry is stocked. It has direct access and a western toilet. The key is behind the number plate."

Hedge shook his hand. "Thank you, old friend."

Evan smiled without speaking, and Dima bowed again. "I suggest you get there soon, and only stay as long as you absolutely must. Ukraine isn't safe for anyone. Especially for spies."

CHAPTER TWELVE

"Do you trust him?" Evan asked as they made a quick circuit of the residential block where the walk-out apartment was located. She studied the windows of the connected flats and of those across the road. They would check out everything on the street before going inside.

"No, but our options are limited right now." Hedge dipped his chin to the only other person on the sidewalk. A middle-aged woman with a grocery sack muttered something and then hurried toward the unit in the middle of the block.

Hedge retrieved the key and opened the door for her. Evan slipped her pistol from her waistband and proceeded to clear the premises before continuing their conversation.

"All good," she said. "But honestly, Hedge, I don't want to just hide here. We need to find out what's going on. We need to find my dad."

"We are definitely not going to hide out here." He clicked on the lights to the studio flat.

Evan scanned the tiny room. Dark curtains that resembled a plaid burlap hung in front of lace panels over the single window to the right of the door. A green sofa that had once been velvet sat at the wall to the left. Two bare bed pillows were stacked at one end, and Evan assumed the couch pulled out into a bed. There was a small table with three chairs against the far wall, with a door to the bathroom beyond the sofa. A short bank of cabinets made up the kitchen, which was really only a hotplate and a cube refrigerator. Dima had said it was stocked. Evan wondered what he meant.

Hedge opened the only cupboard in the kitchen. "There's soup and boxed pasta, I think." He looked into the fridge. "Bottled water. Four eggs."

"Great." Evan flipped the light switch in the bathroom. Toilet, sink, shower, water heater. A towel hung on a rod behind the door. A roll of unbleached toilet paper sat on the back of the tank. "It's fine."

"How are you feeling?" Hedge asked when she returned from the bathroom. He now sat at the table looking through the stuff from the satchel.

"I'm okay. Sore." She shrugged. She longed for a hot bath and a glass of wine, and this place wasn't going to provide that. She knew she wouldn't see either until this mission was over. "Can we get back out and do something? I need to be doing something."

Hedge smiled. "I was just going to ask what you wanted to do next."

"We were heading to the photographer's studio this morning before we were so rudely interrupted. Do you think it's safe to try there again?"

Hedge packed everything back up and reholstered his weapon. "I would love to." He tapped the button on his phone to check the time and then handed Evan the other smartphone. "We should have plenty of time to get there before closing."

A surge of energy invigorated Evan's attitude. Officially, the mission was over, but they weren't even close to being done. Within another minute, they were back on the street, pointed toward the studio.

"How do we play this?" Evan could follow Hedge's lead without much prompting, but she liked to know how to prepare.

Hedge reached out and took her hand. "I think we should try to hire him. We won't get much if we go in asking a bunch of questions. Best if he thinks we're customers."

Evan walked closer. She was safe next to him. He was safer

next to her. Wait. That was with the dress. She had no way to protect him now. A shiver ran down her spine as they walked past the entrance of the Indian restaurant and the studio came into view.

Hedge paused before they approached the door. Evan looked up into his eyes. He almost looked nervous. "Are you ready?"

She nodded. "Good to go."

He opened the door, and a bell clanged loudly against the glass. The front room was the size of a large closet. A small wooden desk sat to the right, flanked on both sides with mismatched chairs. An armchair sat on the left in front of a shelf unit filled with photo albums. Straight ahead was a solid door, painted black. No glass, no handle.

Two seconds later a man in what looked like a fishing vest burst through the door. "Dobryy den'," he boomed. His thunderous voice did not match his pale, slim build.

"Dobryy den'," Hedge responded.

Evan nodded and tried to pronounce the greeting sufficiently. Hedge's grimace told her that she needed practice.

The man motioned for them to sit. He took the chair behind the desk, and Hedge gestured for her to take the other one at the desk while he moved the third to her side. The men began conversing in Ukrainian while she read their body language. Both Hedge and the other man, she caught the name Andriy, looked relaxed and cordial. Andriy asked questions, and Hedge answered. Hedge asked a few questions, and Andriy replied. Everything seemed to be going well until Hedge answered a query with the word *zavtra*.

"Zavtra?" Andriy repeated the word. "Ni. Ne zavtra."

Evan knew that 'ni' meant 'no.' She had no idea about *zavtra*, but it was an emphatic *no* from Andriy.

Hedge didn't back down. He went head-on into negotiations, which Evan surmised involved money. Andriy paused his argument and pulled an agenda from his desk drawer. He flipped through a few pages and frowned, causing deep lines to form on his forehead and chin.

Hedge took Evan's hand in his and kissed her knuckles. She leaned closer and batted her lashes his direction. She wasn't sure why, but it seemed appropriate at the time.

Andriy glanced up and looked her over for the first time. Even with her hair tied up in the scarf and dressed in a too-big men's shirt, he appeared impressed. He shot a doubtful look at Hedge, who shrugged. The men exchanged grins, and then Andriy nodded slowly. Evan didn't know what was being negotiated, but she hoped it wasn't her.

Hedge suddenly held up a finger as if he was getting a message on his phone. He quickly texted someone and then nodded back to Andriy. "Spasybi."

Evan knew that one, too. *Thank you.*

Another minute of questions and answers between the men, another text message. Hedge offered a definitive answer and pulled out a credit card. Andriy wrote in his agenda.

Evan sighed and smiled.

"Spasybi. Spasybi." Hedge nodded toward her as if she should be delighted, so Evan did her best.

The men shook hands over the desk, and then Hedge led her back out to the street.

"And what just happened?" she asked as soon as they rounded the corner.

"We just hired Andriy to photograph our wedding." Hedge pointed to the next block north. "There's a shop up here where we can find you a dress."

"What?!" Evan froze in the middle of the sidewalk.

Hedge stopped and turned to face her. He took both of her hands in his and bowed his head enough to make steady eye contact with her. "Evan Tyler, will you—"

"Stop right there. Don't say another word." Evan shook her head and pressed her lips into a thin line. She drew a deep breath through her nose, trying to control her emotions.

Hedge curled his lip on one side. "I was just kidding. It's for our cover."

Evan blinked and blew her breath out over her lips. "I know. I didn't think you were serious. But in the last two weeks, two men have asked me to marry them. Teo did it as part of our cover, and Cooper as—well, I don't really know why he asked me. All I'm saying is that now they're both dead. Blown up and shot in the head." She swallowed hard. "Just please, please don't ever ask me to marry you. Promise me."

Hedge furrowed his brow. He rubbed his hands over the back of hers. "I promise."

Satisfied, she took another breath and looped her hand over the crook of his elbow. "Okay. We're getting married. And now we're going to find a dress. When is the wedding to be, and where?"

"Zavtra. Tomorrow. Dima has us scheduled with his priest at ten in the morning. The ceremony will take place in a two-hundred-year-old chapel with a beautiful domed top."

Evan laughed. "The wedding is tomorrow? That's zavtra?"

Hedge laughed. "You like that?"

She tossed her head back. "I'm from Texas, dear. Back home, a wedding takes a full six months to orchestrate. Twelve, if you ask my mother."

Pointing to the department store on the corner, Hedge chuckled. "Cover weddings only take twelve hours to execute. So we have a little extra."

"And so I'm going in here and finding whatever dress fits the best, and that will do?" Evan propped her other hand on her hip without thinking, tweaking the bruise on her side.

Hedge tugged her away from the entrance for a second and fixed a severe expression on his face. "First, we have Andriy working for us, which I consider a big victory. We'll get him to talk to us. We'll find out what connection he has to Costa and Cooper and what's going on with all of that. Second, I have seen you dressed in everything from the most brilliant fashion to what you're wearing now. Trust me when I say that you will look beautiful in whatever dress you choose."

Evan watched his face soften. "And is there a third point?"

Hedge blinked. "We're going to find your father. We're going to figure this out." He reached for her hands again. "I'll get you set in the bridal department, and then I'll find a suit."

Her fingers warmed to his touch. She felt calm with him. Safe. The chaos of the day had somehow faded. Shot, chased, betrayed, displaced. All before lunch. Since enjoying the magical borscht, everything seemed to be looking up. By this time to-morrow, she'd be on her cover honeymoon. If they survived the wedding, that is. Zavtra.

She winked at Hedge, hoping he understood that she was good with his plan. "No tuxedo?" she asked as they entered the store.

"Morning wedding. Just a suit." He glanced up to a store map in the marble-lined vestibule, then gestured to his right.

She shook her head. "It still astonishes me that you know all these rules."

"Baby, I'm a catch. You're one lucky lady." Hedge stopped to read a banner on a partition wall ahead. "This way."

They made another right around a display of faceless mannequins, and a sea of white tulle appeared before them.

"I think we're here." Evan took another deep breath. "What's my budget?"

"Do you know how to read the price tags suddenly?" Hedge waved to a clerk.

"No." Evan managed a placid expression as the older woman approached and raised a narrow black brow.

Hedge instructed the woman as to what they wanted. Evan stood like a statue as the woman circled her. She'd been in this situation several times as a fashion model.

The clerk pulled a small notepad from her skirt pocket and scratched out some numbers. She was short and narrow, with unnaturally long fingers that pointed accusingly as she spoke. She seemed disappointed with Evan.

Hedge held up his hands, as if he was surrendering, and then untied the scarf from Evan's head. Her blazing red hair cascaded down her back, and Evan thought she heard the woman gasp.

"Akh, dobre," the clerk said. She now nodded her approval and turned to the dresses against the wall displayed with pink-toned lighting. She asked Hedge another question, holding her pencil ready to write.

"Zavtra," he responded with his most confident tone.

Here it comes.

Or maybe not. Apparently, the tiny woman wasn't shocked by the sudden deadline. Her pace simply quickened as she led the way to her recommended selection.

Hedge leaned close to Evan's ear. "I told her your sizes and that you don't need help in the dressing room. If you do, her name is Sveta. I'll be back here in twenty minutes. Any requests? This is your wedding, too."

"Something that goes with your eyes." Evan looked down and then slowly back up to meet his deep blue gaze. Tiny creases formed at the corners of his eyes, and she knew he was trying to suppress a smile.

"Eef! Eef!" Sveta was snapping her fingers and pointing to the rack of gowns behind her.

"What does *eef* mean?" Evan asked.

Hedge chuckled. "I told her your name was Eve. I think she's calling you. Now get over there and pick a gown."

Evan rolled her eyes and turned away from Hedge. She walked slowly toward Sveta, hoping he was watching her.

Finding a wedding gown was something she'd imagined for years. She'd worn wedding gowns in fashion shows several times. Each one made her think of what she would someday choose. She'd take her mother and best friend with her. They would spend the whole day trying on dresses.

But momma wasn't here. And her best friend was in the next department picking out a suit. Sveta would have to do, and right now she was frantically pulling out gowns and making ooh and ahh sounds in Ukrainian.

Evan picked up the first one Sveta offered. The strapless bust sparkled with sequins. The silhouette was form-fitting down to the knees followed by an explosion of tulle netting.

"Ni," Evan said in her most polite rejection. With her long red hair, the last thing she wanted was to look like the Little Mermaid.

Sveta held out another. This one had potential. The main gown had a solid, strapless bodice and a chiffon overlay with shirring at the ribs and sleeves. The skirt was full and layered. The perfect camouflage for her sidearm.

"Dah," Evan said with a nod.

"Dobre." Sveta pulled down another. The second was similar in style, but the overlay was lace instead of sheer chiffon.

Evan decided to try both. She followed Sveta to the dressing room. Sveta hung the gowns on wall hooks and gestured to a velvet bench on the other side of the small room. A full-length mirror hung on the back of the door. It wasn't nearly enough for a proper examination, but it didn't really matter to Evan. This was all just for show.

"Spasybi," Evan said as Sveta closed the door behind her. *Let's do this.*

She pulled off her shirts slowly and carefully, trying not to twist at her bruised ribs. She folded them into a neat square and placed them on the bench. She looked at herself in the mirror. Her right side ribcage resembled a tie-dyed tee shirt. A blossom of colors covered her otherwise porcelain skin. Purple, blue, green, and yellow glowed like a kaleidoscope in the fluorescent overhead lighting.

She pulled her Springfield pistol from her waistband and tucked it between the shirts. Before pulling off her blue jeans, she checked the pockets and found her earrings. It was safe to put them back in. Nothing would be connected to her ear receiver now. She slipped the silver studs back into her earlobes and continued undressing. The jeans went on top of the other clothes.

Evan wasn't wearing the right underwear or shoes for a wedding gown. *Momma would be ashamed.* Never go into a dressing room without the proper accessories for the outfit. Every decent young woman knows this rule. *Just ask Momma.*

The lace gown was first. Evan unzipped the back and stepped into the pool of white lace. She pulled it up around her ribs and bust, careful not to snag anything as she slipped her arms into the sleeves. Lovely. The fit was nearly perfect. Snug but not tight. The overlay had a slight stretch to it, which was fine, but it caused the sleeves to ride up and sit just above her elbows.

Evan studied the fit in the mirror. "Ni. Not quite." It would work if the other one didn't. After all, this was just make-believe.

She carefully removed the lace gown and clipped it back on the hanger. Now for the chiffon number. It went on easily and fit the same as the other gown, except that the shirred sleeves stayed in place. Better.

"Eef?" Sveta knocked on her door. "Eef?"

Evan opened the door, and Sveta stood in the hall holding a short veil in one hand and a tiara in the other. She gasped and smiled.

"Ni, ni, ni," she said and placed the headpieces on a folding chair nearby. She grabbed Evan's hand and pulled her out of the dressing room and to a well-lit triple mirror.

Evan didn't understand a single word Sveta was saying, but when she saw herself in the mirror, she knew. This was the dress.

If there had been any doubt, it dissolved the moment she saw Hedge standing behind her, looking like he might melt.

Sveta hurried to his side, and they struck up another conversation. Hedge blinked and nodded. He clearly approved. "Go change, and I'll take care of everything out here."

Evan was out of the gown and back into her jeans in another two minutes. They found the lingerie and shoe departments next and were back at the flat within the hour.

"I'm gonna pass out, Hedge." Evan held the side of her head as she went into the bathroom to prepare for bed.

"Don't you want anything to eat?" Hedge arranged the garment bags on the curtain rod over the window. "There's soup."

"Ni." She rolled her shoulders as she undressed and turned on the shower. "When I get out, I'll drink some water. That's all I want."

Hedge laughed. "Big day tomorrow."

She called back to him from under the tepid spray of the shower. "Zavtra!"

CHAPTER THIRTEEN

Hedge sat at the table in the shabby apartment watching Evan sleep. The early morning sunlight was starting to glow through the curtains, outlining the wedding clothes hanging from the rod. *What was he doing?*

He had her bed ready for her before she was finished in the bathroom. When it was his turn, he'd taken a little extra time than he needed, to make sure she was asleep when he came out. Less temptation.

He'd tried to keep everything professional with her, but he knew it was just a matter of time. From the moment he met her, he knew that he was lost. *No, saved.* She was smart and fast. Her eyes flashed with unspoken innuendo. He couldn't tell sometimes if she was overly confident or extremely naïve. He suspected it was a little of both. She got his humor. *Face it, buddy, she's got all of you.*

He had spent the last month pushing her away and then pulling her back. And then pushing her away again. But now they were alone together. She was all he had left, and he was all she had. He didn't want to let her down. He couldn't bear it.

A wedding was his first thought when they got to the photography studio. As he listened to her purring in that dream-state just before waking, he couldn't decide if he should call the plan off of go through with it. Cruel. A pretend wedding when they both just wanted to be together. But that wasn't all she wanted. She needed to find her father. They both needed to find him. Gordon Tyler was their best hope to straightening out this fiasco.

Evan started to stir. He stood and moved to the kitchen-ette to start a kettle of water to boil for tea. He wanted coffee, but this was what they had.

"You didn't wake me up," she said as she sat up in the pull-out bed. The ancient mattress springs squeaked when she stood and crossed to the bathroom. She wore only her tee shirt and panties.

Hedge averted his eyes, focusing instead on the hotplate. He waited until she closed the door. "I wanted you to get as much sleep as possible." He didn't hear any response. "How are you feeling?"

"I'll live." She returned with the right side of her shirt raised so that he could inspect her ribs. Her voice was warm and suggestive. "What do you think?"

The bruising was as bad as he'd ever seen with body armor. Worse than he'd experienced. He knew Evan was in pain. He winced at the thought. "Maybe later we can get you some meds."

"I'm fine. Really." Her tone cooled, and she lowered her shirt.

Evan seemed to notice that he was making an effort not to take her in his arms and, well, he had a hundred different ideas about what he'd like to do. But he wasn't going to do any of those things. He was going to keep her safe, at least from him. For now.

She turned away from him and sat on the edge of the bed. "I wanted to ask you about this wedding thing."

Here it comes. She was going to ask why. She probably had been analyzing the whole idea in her sleep. She was going to tease him, throw herself at him, or something worse—which would be anything else. "Yeah?" He tried to act nonchalant.

"Do we dress in our wedding clothes here or at the church?"

She was an angel. He sighed and nodded. "Probably we should go ahead and dress here. Dima is sending a car for us at nine. He's got all the paperwork ready. Probably an envelope of cash, too, for the priest."

"What kind of paperwork?" Evan stood back up and started tucking the linens around the mattress.

"Well, he got us a real priest, so it has to look official, even if it's not. A real priest won't intentionally conduct a fake ceremony." Hedge helped her fold the bed away, and the sofa was back. Evan sat with one foot tucked under her.

"But he'll take an envelope of cash?" Evan raised her perfectly arched brows.

"A charitable donation." Hedge laughed and pulled the kettle off the burner just as it started to whistle. "You want some tea?"

"Yeah." Evan punched the button on her phone. "I tried to call my dad again last night. No answer. Nothing from him."

"We'll find him."

"I hope so." She jumped up. "It's nearly eight o'clock! Did you say the car would be here at nine?"

"Yes." Hedge poured out two cups of water and dropped a teabag in each. "Don't panic. You can change clothes faster than anyone I've ever seen."

Evan grabbed the cup from his hand and took a sip before the tea had a chance to steep or cool. "Too hot." She blew over the cup and set it on the table. "Yeah, but I gotta put on a bride face. We want Andriy to believe this is all real. I can't go to church looking like this."

She disappeared back into the bathroom. Hedge picked up his teacup automatically and sipped, scalding his tongue. "It is too hot." He raked his hands through his hair. "And you look perfectly lovely to me."

Twenty minutes later, Hedge was dressed in his shirt and slacks. He sat on the sofa to pull on a pair of black cashmere socks and tie the black patent brogues. His peacock blue tie hung loosely over his shoulders, and only his jacket remained on the hanger.

Evan came out of the bathroom looking like a goddess. She'd pinned her hair up in front and left her long curls loose down the back. Her makeup was cover model perfect. She now wore the pearl white strapless corset, panties, and stockings they had purchased for the occasion.

Hedge didn't dare look for too long. "Will you need help getting into the gown or can you do it by yourself?"

Evan grinned at him. "I can do it. If you don't want to help, that is."

He grabbed both ends of his necktie. Did he dare joke? "I can help, but it might take you longer if I do."

She only flashed her wicked grin. "Is there anything for breakfast. I want to get something in my tummy before I dress."

Hedge handed her a plate of scrambled egg. "Here's a little protein for you. I wasn't sure how you liked your eggs."

"Scrambled is great." She cleaned the plate in five bites or so. She licked the back of the fork and set the plate neatly stacked upon Hedge's empty to the side of the hotplate. Hedge watched her as she turned to face the gown.

He had removed the dress from the garment bag while she was still asleep, and it hung from the curtain rod like a shimmering cloud. Evan appeared to be more intimidated by this white gown than she'd been by the Little Black Dress. This outfit had no body armor, no hidden cameras, no secret pulses or sensors. It was candlelight taffeta and chiffon. Evan looked terrified.

"Are you okay?" Hedge tugged on his sleeves as he buttoned the cuffs. "Offer to help you dress still stands."

"I can do it." She hadn't moved. "It's just weird, you know?"

Hedge tried to downplay the situation. "You've worn wedding dresses before."

She nodded. "I have. But on a catwalk. For a show. Not to a church."

"It's still a show." He wished he didn't have to say those words. "Let me help you step into it."

Evan grimaced and moved aside. He took the hanger down and carefully laid the skirt out to make a hole with the bodice. Evan stepped one stockinged foot through, and then the other. She took hold of the sides and lifted it into place. Hedge held the waistband gently around her middle until she was able to slide her arms through the sleeves. She turned away from him, and he pulled the zipper up and straightened the sash to lay flat down the back of the skirt.

She spun to face him, and his heart almost exploded.

"Does it look all right?" she asked.

Rather, he assumed that's what she asked. Her perfect pink lips moved to shape those words, but he couldn't hear anything but his heart pounding in his ears.

He regained presence of mind and smiled, though he was sure he'd been wearing a goofy grin for the last twenty minutes. "You don't like it when I call you perfect."

Evan raised and lowered her lashes a few times. She did that sometimes, and Hedge loved it. He didn't know if she was trying to manipulate him or not. Right now he didn't care. Her gaze shifted to his tie, and she reached to button his collar closed. "I thought I told you to get a tie that matched your eyes. This one has a smidge too much green."

Hedge held his chin up and let her tie the half Windsor. "Maybe I wanted to match the color of your eyes." He had his hands around her waist. He pulled her closer, and her lips parted slightly just an inch from his.

A car honked outside, causing them both to jump.

"I still have to put on my shoes." Evan looked around the room for the silk pumps. "And you need your jacket."

Hedge pulled back the curtain and waved to the driver. The long black car was festooned with white ribbons, sunflowers, and poppies from bumper to bumper.

Turning back to Evan, "I have my pistol and extra ammo. Do you have everything you need?"

Evan sat down to put on her shoes and then strapped on her thigh holster. She secured her weapon in place. "Good to go, sir."

"Then, my beautiful bride," he said, buttoning his jacket. "Our chariot awaits."

CHAPTER FOURTEEN

The stark white plaster of the refectory church matched the grand cathedral that towered just a few dozen meters away. Both buildings were topped with green tile roofs, gold domes, and gilt Eastern Orthodox crosses pointing to the heavens. Both buildings welcomed visitors through ancient wooden doors. Evan entered the refectory and stopped in place. Every inch of the building, from the glossy granite tile floors to the soaring arches separating the different rooms, dazzled Evan's senses.

The dark-stained wood was almost black with age. Brightly painted icons with golden backgrounds lined each side wall, leading from the entrance, through the nave, up to the sanctuary arch. Candles flickered in front of each icon, giving the slightest appearance that the carvings moved on their own. A shiver ran down Evan's back.

"Where will the ceremony be?" she asked Hedge, looking for pews and an altar.

"Right here. Or up there." He pointed to the intricately carved arch ahead of them.

She glanced around the room. Several tourists wandered from saint to saint, lighting candles and murmuring prayers. "But where do people sit?"

"They don't." Hedge nodded as the priest entered through a side door near the sanctuary. The door behind them opened again. Andriy came in and raised a hand in their direction. Hedge nudged her elbow. "I'll go talk to the priest for a moment. You go back outside with Andryi for a few photos. He won't be allowed to take anything within the church. But we can see if he's meeting anyone here or if he has anyone set up in the gardens." He squeezed her shoulder. "Keep your eyes open."

Evan watched Hedge approach the priest. He would take care of the paperwork and manage whatever other details might come up. She could handle Andryi. If there was one personality she understood well, it was photographers.

Back out in the bright sunlight, Andryi seemed focused on getting plenty of good pictures. "Dah. Dah," he said with each shutter click. He took several of Evan posing in front of the wooden doors before leading her to the black iron gazebo in the middle of the garden.

Evan didn't understand the words of his instructions, but when he tapped on her shoulder or pointed to her chin, she knew exactly how to move to make him smile and nod, clicking one photo after another. She scanned the area, but nobody looked out of place. A few tourists gathered to watch her photo session, but no one seemed overly interested.

Andryi led her to stand in front of the beautiful bell tower. The building rose as an arched gate into the complex. Painted blue and white plaster, it resembled a four-tiered wedding cake, with a gold dome topper. The photographer motioned for her to stand in the archway, letting the direct sunlight cut into the dark shadow across her face. Andryi repositioned her hair to fall over her shoulder. He took several photos there before changing his roll of film.

He said something in Russian and then gestured for them to return to the church. Evan nodded when she saw Hedge watching from the open doors. It was time.

The priest wore black and white robes with a gold embroidered mantle and cap. Another man, this one without head covering, stood at his side, in front of a draped table. Evan guessed he was a deacon. The priest made a quick announcement to the room, and the small crowd of tourists congregated around them. He offered both Evan and Hedge a lit taper candle. Evan watched Hedge take his, and she did the same.

The priest began reading from Scripture, and when he

paused, a small choir of five or six singers responded with a short verse. Evan was so engrossed in the ceremony, she hadn't noticed when the singers came in.

The priest continued, always followed with a choral response. She wondered if the priest was speaking Russian, Ukrainian, or Greek with a heavy accent. Whatever it was, she didn't understand more than *amen*, which sounded like ah-meen. She peeked at Hedge from the corner of her eye to see him say, "amen," and realized that everyone but her was amen-ing.

After several minutes of chanting, singing, and prayer, the priest made a cross in front of Hedge, and then in front of her, and then another between them. The deacon picked up a gold crown from the table and handed it to the priest. He said a blessing over it and held it out toward Hedge, who kissed the band before the priest placed it on Hedge's head. The priest repeated the blessing twice more before turning to Evan. The pressure was on.

She turned to face the priest, and he was holding out a crown for her to kiss, too. She did, and as the priest blessed it twice more, it was placed on her head. This was unlike any West Texas wedding she'd been to before.

Another question from the priest, to which Hedge answered, "Dah." He turned to face Evan, placing his candle free right hand over hers.

Another cross formed between them, as the priest said something to Hedge and then Evan. Another blessing. Another prayer. Another amen.

The deacon took Hedge's crown while the priest chanted. He did the same for Evan. Hedge puffed out his candle and nodded. Evan followed. The ribbon of white smoke drifted up through the arches like a prayer.

While the deacon took the candles, the priest stacked the couple's hands on top of his and placed one end of his mantle over the stack. He led them both in a circle around the table. Removing the mantle, he chanted another prayer. Another amen. This one sounded more final.

The priest's voice seemed to relax, though he held up his hands to the congregation as if instructing them to be patient. He asked Hedge a question. Both men nodded to each other, and Hedge led Evan a few steps to the side of the room.

In a calm, clear voice, Hedge began. "I, Hedgewick Odysseus Parker, take you, Evangeline Dale Tyler, to be my partner in this great adventure."

Evan nearly swallowed her tongue. She could barely get past his name, not to mention that she was about to have to offer her own vows when he was finished. Her heart pounded in her ears. She needed to pay attention. She looked up into Hedge's ocean blue eyes as he continued.

"I promise to stay by your side, no matter what challenges we face. To protect you with my life. To always have your back. I will show you respect and value your opinion, even if it is different from mine. I will, to the best of my ability, provide whatever you need, physically, emotionally, and spiritually. I vow all these things before God and man, for as long as we both live." His voice was steady. He never broke eye-contact.

Evan struggled to hear over her heart thumping loudly in her ears. She waited for a second, unsure if the priest had something to say about it. He didn't.

"It's your turn," Hedge whispered.

He suddenly looked nervous. *Was he nervous?*

She drew a deep breath. "I, Evangeline Dale Tyler, take you, Hedgewick Odysseus Parker." She paused for a second, to be sure she had said it correctly. He nodded. "To be my partner in this amazing adventure." *Was she supposed to repeat everything he had said? Could she even remember it all? Focus, girl.* She stared into his eyes, and he smiled.

"I promise to stay with you through good times and bad. To protect you, to care for you, and to respect you. I promise to value you in every way. I promise to listen to you. I will share with you everything I have and everything I am." She tried to remember his words, but all she could see was his expression. His eyes seemed to glisten, but maybe that was the candlelight from around the room. "I vow all these things before God and man, for as long as we both live." She knew this was supposed to be just a show, but in the depths of her heart, she couldn't have been more sincere.

The couple returned to their place in front of the priest, who spoke again to the small congregation and offered another blessing. The deacon organized a receiving line from one side. Evan noticed two men leaving the chapel through the main doors and another exiting through a side door. She glanced at Hedge, who acknowledged with a nod.

After a few minutes of cheek kisses, congratulations, and *vitayu*, Andriy soon approached and led them outside to the front doors, where he began snapping more pictures. After a few dozen with Evan and Hedge together in the garden, Andriy gestured to their car.

Andriy and Hedge spoke with the driver of their car, and soon they were all on the way to a park.

Evan blew out a deep breath once they were in the car. She wanted to have a quick chat with Hedge about their ceremony, but the job seemed to be the top priority. "You saw the people leaving?"

Hedge nodded. "I did. Did you get a good look at any of them?"

"No. It was too dark. I hoped you had. I'm not even one hundred percent sure that all three were men." She sighed. "The Little Black Dress would come in pretty handy right now."

"I'm sure they were all men, but I don't know if we should

be concerned or not." He rolled his shoulders back in a stretch. "They could have been tourists. They saw a wedding, and when it was over, they left."

"Could be." Evan nodded. "Is that what your gut is saying?"

"No."

"Mine neither."

Evan gestured to the car in front of theirs. "And what about Andriy? Is he just a wedding photographer? Is he more than that?"

Hedge clicked his tongue. "Andriy is more challenging to read. Why would Costa or Cooper need him? I mean, you've worked with photographers before."

She rolled her eyes. "Hundreds of photogs."

"And he's legitimate?"

"Yeah, he was picky about how I stood, and lighting, and all of it." Evan shrugged. "Your name is really Hedgewick Odysseus?" She flashed the biggest smile she could manage. "I *thought* Hedge was a nickname."

"So now you know the truth." Hedge stretched his arm across her shoulders.

Evan rocked her head back into the bend of his elbow. "I guess your momma had some mighty big plans for you, right from the start."

"My grandfathers' names. Big shoes to fill on both sides."

The car slowed to a stop. Andriy waited for them on the sidewalk, motioning for them to follow him to an angel statue. They reached the stone figure at the same time as another bride and groom. Andriy insisted the other couple and their photographer go first.

Andriy scanned the park for another vignette. As they moved toward an arbor of red roses, Evan noticed another wedding party in the distance. A thought struck her.

She leaned close to Hedge's ear. "Andriy is Costa's LBD."

"What do you mean?" Hedge kept his voice low and barely moved his lips.

"He can take pictures of anyone, anywhere, and nobody notices him. He might even be wired for sound, and for all we know, he might understand everything we've been saying." As Evan finished her sentence, Andriy froze in place in front of them.

Hedge took a half-step in front of Evan. "Stop," he whispered.

Andriy turned to face them for a split second and then took off across the park at full speed toward his car.

Hedge followed close behind, and Evan tried, but running in a full-skirted wedding gown and heels proved to be harder than she expected. By the time she got back to their car, Andriy had already ripped into traffic in his own vehicle.

Evan lept into the back seat as Hedge ordered their driver to keep up with Andriy at all costs.

"I wish I'd picked sneakers for under the dress. Three-inch heels aren't practical for a chase."

Hedge pulled his tie loose and checked his weapon. "Get out your Springfield. You may need it."

"Yessir." Evan inhaled a deep breath, wincing through the pain of her ribcage. She pulled up the layers of chiffon and unholstered her pistol. She checked the round in the chamber and nodded. "Ready."

Hedge shouted something at the driver who punched the accelerator and whipped the black car from one lane to another. Flowers flew off, and ribbons fluttered furiously behind them. Evan and Hedge had to brace themselves to keep from flying into one another's laps. In seconds, their car had caught up to

Andriy's.

"I'm going to try to take a tire," Hedge said, rolling down a window.

Before he had the chance, Andriy made a sharp turn onto a side street. As they turned to follow, another car clipped their rear bumper, causing their vehicle to fish-tail. Their driver shook his head and gunned the engine again. He muttered something that Evan surmised was a level-one swear. He maneuvered the sedan through the narrow street until he'd caught up with Andriy again.

Andriy's car entered a larger intersection and was t-boned by a delivery van. Several cars stopped, blocking the road in every direction. Evan held her breath, waiting to see if anyone was hurt.

She saw Andriy hop out of his wrecked car and turn toward them. He raised his pistol and began firing.

"Get down," Hedge yelled, pushing her to the floorboard.

She felt and heard at least one of their tires blow over the sound of bullets hitting their engine and shattering the windshield. The popping sounds stopped, and she raised her head enough to evaluate the situation. Hedge was standing beside their car with his weapon raised.

"Come on. We have to catch him." He reached inside for her hand. "Kick off your shoes. Let's go."

Evan clambered out of the back seat and saw their driver, shot through the head and chest. Steam and smoke plumed from the new holes in the hood of the car. Her stomach churned, and her side throbbed, but she felt a fresh surge of adrenaline pulsing through her system.

This was not how she imagined her wedding day.

CHAPTER FIFTEEN

Hedge and Evan raced down the black granite streets after Andriy, keeping their weapons tucked at their sides. Hedge focused on keeping Andriy in view, but couldn't help but worry about Evan. She was still recovering from badly bruised ribs and now forced to run in stocking feet. He turned to check on her and was amazed to see that she was only half a step behind him.

They dodged pedestrians and raced cautiously across intersections. Drivers in Kyiv were always careful to allow foot traffic the right of way, and that helped, but Andriy ran with seemingly no destination in mind. They chased him in a full two-block loop before he finally ducked into a small machine repair shop.

Hedge slowed as he approached the storefront and motioned for Evan to stay behind him. Andriy might have kept running through the building, but Hedge couldn't be sure.

"I'm going in," he barked to Evan.

"Right behind you."

Hedge readied his sidearm and took a step into view of the large window. Through the glare of the glass, he saw Andriy, flanked by two of the men who left the wedding chapel earlier. All three had their weapons raised. In a split second, the plate glass window shattered. Hedge lunged back to Evan's side.

"Go," he ordered. "He's got friends."

"Where to?" Evan asked between breaths.

Hedge swept her in front of him. He looked back to see the men running after them. "Run toward the metro. It's another block ahead and across the street." He looked back again. He saw the men getting into a blue sedan. "Cross here and run as fast as you can. They've got wheels."

Evan glanced over her shoulder and nodded. "The metro? Are you sure?"

"Easier to hide. Fastest way to put distance between them and us." He noticed she was slowing. Her breathing sounded labored.

"I thought," she said, panting, "that we... were chasing them."

Hedge scooped his arm under her shoulder blades and urged her physically. "That was before. They outnumber us and outgun us. We need to regroup."

He pulled her up the steps to the subway terminal and through the doors. Once inside, he stood in front of her as she holstered her weapon back to her thigh.

"I'm in a big puffy wedding dress." She said with a marked rattle in her voice. "I kinda stand out. I'll hide in a ladies' room, and you go on. You can come back for me in an hour or two."

Hedge growled. "Were you not paying attention back in the church? I'm not leaving you. Get your fluffy white butt down that escalator. Do you understand?"

"Yessir." She took a deep breath and pushed her shoulders back.

As they hurried through the turnstiles, Hedge noticed the men bursting through the entry doors. He nudged Evan. "They're behind us. Move as quickly as you can."

Evan rushed, without running, to the head of the escalator. She paused and turned. "This stupid skirt is too big. Help me pull some of these layers off."

She was a genius. "Raise your arms up just a little," Hedge said. He grabbed the top layers of chiffon fabric and pulled straight down from the sash. The sheer fabric pulled away from the taffeta underskirt, and Hedge lifted the billowing fabric over her head and tossed it behind them as they reached the bottom landing where the steps disappeared into the mechanism. They ran to the next escalator, heading toward the trains.

The yards of white fabric quickly jammed the mechanics of the moving steps, causing people to stop in a glut at the top of the stairs. As they descended the next escalator, Hedge grabbed the sash itself and pulled it from the dress. He tossed it on the downward stairs, hoping to cause it to stop as well. Instead, the riders simply picked it up and dropped it over a lighted sign on the median between the walkways.

As the bottom of the first tier of escalators came into view, Hedge leaned forward to whisper in Evan's ear. "I'm going to need a little more fabric from you, Honey." He grabbed her skirt at knee level and ripped. The mid-weight taffeta made a satisfying zipping sound as Hedge converted her full-length gown into a midi. As Evan stepped off the escalator, Hedge threw the bundle of taffeta on the disappearing steps. The jammed mechanism ground to a halt. The angled tunnels were suddenly filled with Ukrainian curses. They could hear their pursuers clattering down the frozen steps above.

Hedge hated to cause this kind of destruction, but Andriy and his friends were gaining on them, and he had to get Evan to safety. He picked up speed, pulling her toward the train platform, dodging others moving up and down the long passageway.

Soon they had reached the platform areas. Evan stopped to study the maps on the wall.

"Which one do we take?" she asked.

Hedge pointed to the arch ahead on the left. "Run as far and as fast as you can until you see one that is about to board. That's the one we want."She glared up at him. "We're getting on the first random train we can?"

Hedge nodded as they ran. "They can't guess where we're going if we don't know, either." They weaved through crowds, making busy people angry. He heard Evan's voice.

"Excuse us. So sorry."

He squeezed her arm and shot her a warning glance. Apologizing in English was just making people more upset. "Pereproshuyu." He tried to say it loud enough for her to hear and repeat if she absolutely had to. Texans were a little too nice for Eastern Europe.

The screech of an approaching train sounded just ahead. Hedge looped his arm around her waist and cinched her to his side. He pushed forward until they were only one big step from the yellow boarding line. He looked around but couldn't see Andriy or his friends.

As the train flew into place and howled to a stop, the crowds on the platform crushed forward, into the car as a wave of people pushed out. Hedge did his best to keep hold of her, but Evan started slipping from his grasp.

"Help, Hedge!" she cried.

They only had seconds to make it onto the train, and someone else had hold of his partner. He looked into the eyes of one of Andriy's sidekicks. The man grinned, pulling on Evan's arm. She was in limbo, being stretched like a wishbone over the threshold of the train door.

He doubled down on his grip, knowing that he was crushing her injured ribs. Hedge planted his foot behind her and twisted, practically tossing her into the car. With his other leg, he kicked outward, knocking the man loose. The heel of his shoe crashed into the closing door and came off his foot. It did not make it inside.

"Are you okay?" he asked Evan. They were both wedged into the car, unable to step in any farther.

"Yeah," she answered.

Hedge studied her face for a second. She wasn't okay. Tears

pooled in her eyes, and her complexion was blotchy. He didn't know if she was going to throw up or faint. He scanned the faces of the people around them. He didn't recognize any of them, but that really didn't mean anything. Anyone could have a knife, a needle, a club.

He held Evan close to his side. "I'm sorry." He whispered. "We'll get off at the next stop."

She blinked a few times, and the color started to even across her face again. "If I wasn't here, would you get off at the next stop?"

He didn't think he would. That's what Andriy would probably expect. "I don't know what I would do if you weren't with me."

"Yes, you do." She took a deep breath and leaned heavily into his grip. "Whatever that is, that's what we'll do. I am fine. I'm hurting, but I'm not incapacitated. I can keep up with you. Especially now that you only have one shoe." She smiled.

"You're more than capable. I know that." He stepped out of his remaining shoe and kicked it under the nearest bench seat. "Now we're even."

She laughed as another train screamed past them, inches away on the sister track. "No, you just gave the advantage back to me."

All he wanted to do was kiss her. "Okay, then, prove it. At the next stop, I want to see you get off, run down to the very next door, and get back on. Same train, okay?"

Evan rolled her shoulders and narrowed her eyes. Her expression was a cold steel smirk.

Hedge loosened his grip slightly, and they both turned to face the doorway. The car bumped more forcefully as it entered the next station. They only had about eight seconds to make their move.

The train lurched to a stop. The doors slid open. Hedge and Evan pushed forward with all their might. The other passengers moved quickly to the archways beyond the platform. Evan and Hedge turned a sharp left and melted back into the crowd loading onto the train. Just as they got on, Hedge caught a glimpse of Andriy. He was watching them pull away, and he was talking on his phone.

"Did you see him?" Evan asked. "Chances are, Andriy was phoning someone at the next stop."

Hedge nodded. "You're right about that." He snugged his arm around her shoulders. "What do you think we should do?"

Evan shook her head. "I suppose getting off before the next stop is out of the question?"

Hedge laughed. "That's great, but it's not really an option."

He looked around the train car. Above the windows were signs noting train routes, advertisements for everything from toilets to candy, and emergency evacuation procedures. His eyes found what he was looking for.

"Let's move to the next car." He gestured over Evan's shoulder to the door at the end of the carriage.

They slithered between the other passengers until they got to the connector doors. Hedge gestured discreetly to a steel lever with a round, red handle. Evan's brow raised and her eyes grew wide.

"What?" she whispered. Her lips barely moved. "I was only kidding."

Hedge nodded. "I know. It's not quite what you think. We'll wait until we're almost back to the platform. We just need a few seconds."

The car started bouncing feverishly. Hedge moved into position, keeping a tight grip on Evan's hand. He waited until the passengers began shuffling toward the side doors. The lights flickered as the train reached the station. Once inside, Hedge reached up and tugged the lever downward. The whole transport bumped as the brakes squealed to a premature stop. The doors slid open, still in the shadows of the tunnel.

Travelers muttered and whined as many poured out onto the narrow walkway. Others stayed in place, waiting the extra minute for the train to resume its travels. They were still fifty meters from the first platform, even farther to their designated destination. Hedge and Evan slipped through the connector door, and then into the dark tunnel.

He waited for the crowd to clear. "Let's see if we can find a maintenance closet. We can hold there for a bit."

Evan and Hedge limped to a tunnel alcove, and Hedge pushed the door open. They got the door closed behind them and then started searching the walls for a light switch.

"You feel anything on that side?" Hedge asked.

"No switch here. I think I found a shelf unit, though." Evan's voice echoed in the narrow concrete room.

"Let me check overhead." He felt a ball chain dangling above them and pulled. A dim bulb popped to life, casting a yellow-orange glow around them. "Found it."

Evan had a tight grip on his jacket, and Hedge suspected she was struggling with her pain. He scanned the tiny room. The shelves behind Evan contained a short stack of Russian manuals for subway upkeep. From the dust and grime covering them, Hedge surmised nobody had been in the room for years. A few empty cans lined the back wall. A blackened towel hung on a hook on the back of the door. Hedge started to pull it down, but even off the hook, the towel maintained its shape.

"Eww." Evan cringed. "Don't touch that."

Hedge let it fall to the floor. It bent on impact and broke in half. Evan started to laugh, which soon turned to a moan.

"We need to get you someplace safe. You're too hurt to keep up like this." He held her face in his hands. Creases were deepening on her forehead and chin.

The light flickered, and the halted train outside now shrieked back to life. It echoed through the tunnel as it moved on to the destination platform.

"I feel safe right here." She slipped her arms under his jacket and around his waist.

Hedge inched his fingers into her auburn tresses, pulling down her updo until her hair fell in loose curls around her face. He combed through the red silken waves with his fingers, arranging them around her shoulders. With a handful of hair in his right hand, he pulled her closer with his left.

He lifted Evan's face to his and covered her lips with his. He released her after several seconds. He needed a breath to clear his mind, and he felt something strange in his hand.

"What is this?" he asked, trying to see the small object stuck to his finger.

"It's called a kiss. Apparently, that priest didn't know about them either. He didn't even have you kiss the bride." Evan took a step back when Hedge didn't respond. "What is that?"

Hedge held his hand up toward the struggling light bulb. His eyes strained. It was a metallic square, flat, about the size of a small fly.

"Oh no." He recognized it. He held it down where Evan could see. "Did Andriy touch your hair today?"

"Yeah. A couple of times." Her expression changed when she saw it. "It's a micro-tracker?"

He nodded. "They probably know we're in here."

Evan reached under her skirt for her Springfield. "Then I suppose it's time for us to go. You ready?"

Hedge pulled his weapon from his holster. He leaned forward and kissed her again. "Let's go."

CHAPTER SIXTEEN

Rowan Kirk pressed his body flat against the cold wall tiles in the corner of the wheelchair-accessible stall in the men's room. It was the one place in InDIGO Headquarters, the only sixteen cubic feet of space, where there was no possibility of being recorded visually or audibly. It disturbed him to know this fact, but in an ultra-high security government facility, it paid to be an IT geek.

He adjusted the settings on his smartphone to initiate his app. He had written the code with precise encryption for his own personal program. He had hoped he would never need the program at all. It was absurd to imagine it. But here he stood in the bathroom, trying to activate it.

Eleven seconds for the first ping. Europe. Fourteen seconds for the second ping. Ukraine. They're still in Ukraine. Why are they still in Ukraine? Eighteen seconds for the third ping. Kyiv. Why in the world are they still in Kyiv? He started the fourth ping.

"Kirk?" It was Eleanor McKinnon-Grey's Georgia peach voice. "Kirk, are you in here?"

"No." He punched his abort button, mid-ping. He dropped his phone into his shirt pocket and reached over to flush the toilet.

"Well, okay." Elle's tone was stronger. She was no longer standing at the door. She was in the room. "Fischer called a meeting in the conference room in five minutes. Anyone not at the meeting will be taken into custody and have their clearance revoked indefinitely." She smiled as he came out of the stall. "I just thought you might like to join this one."

Kirk went to the sink to wash his hands. "I didn't get that

message." His phone buzzed in his pocket. "That's probably it now."

Elle leaned over the sink and whispered. "You haven't been in touch with any of our favorite people, have you?"

Kirk stood up straight and looked directly into the LED fixture over the wall mirror. Women speaking to him, in general, made him nervous. Even good friends like Elle. Women asking him questions which necessitated deceptive responses made him even more nervous.

"You ordered me not to contact them." This was not a lie.

"That's right." She handed him a paper towel from the wall dispenser. "And you have obeyed?"

"I respect your authority," he said. Again, not a lie. He tossed the paper towel into the trash bin and gestured toward the door. "Why do you ask?"

Elle didn't move. "Because, I happen to know that Fischer will be confiscating everyone's phones, tablets, and notebooks. He is desperate to find the mole here. If someone were to have traces of communication with our friends on their devices, or if someone fails to turn in a device, they will be taken into custody immediately. I assumed you might want this information. I know how you like to be prepared."

Kirk retrieved his phone from his pocket and punched a button on the side. He held it down for three seconds. It made a simple power-off sound. He smiled and returned the phone to his pocket. "I'm ready. Thanks for the heads up."

She allowed Kirk to hold the men's room door open for her and led him toward the conference room. "No problem, whatsoever."

They stopped at his desk long enough to pick up Kirk's other devices. "I suppose you've already relinquished yours?" he asked her.

Elle tilted her head and offered a short sigh. "That sounded a little like an accusation. I'm not a traitor to Hedge and Evan any more than they are to us. You know that."

He did.

"We're all just trying to bring them home safely." Elle furrowed her brow and lowered her tone. "And Fischer knows we're the best bet in getting that done."

Kirk sniffed and muttered under his breath. "He also knows we're the least likely to share what we find. At least I am, considering my own personal encounter with Xandra. My shoulder still hurts."

Max Fischer cleared his throat and gestured to a twenty-something woman sitting at a long table at the far side of the room. "Agent Kirk, would you be so kind as to power up all your equipment, log in, and turn everything over to Ms. Falstaff, please?"

Kirk carried over his laptop and opened it up. He went through the process of keying in a PIN and scanning his thumb to bring up his home screen. "I'll need to unlock the individual programs. This will just take a moment."

The young woman sat back in her plastic folding chair and looked astonished at the variety of security features Kirk had set on each of his programs. Some required passwords. Some unlocked with facial recognition scans. The LBD main program required a nine-point geometric pattern match.

"Is that all?" the woman asked.

Kirk rolled his eyes. "On the laptop, yes." He then handed her his tablet and smartphone, unlocking them each with only his fingerprint.

The woman took them and placed them in front of the laptop. "All that for your notebook and practically nothing for the others?"

"Agent Falstaff." Kirk checked her badge to be sure. "What security measures do you have on your phone?"

She blinked and shrugged. "Same. A fingerprint scan."

"And have you ever been hacked?" Kirk crossed his arms over his chest. He knew by challenging her, she would probably not push him further.

"No, sir."

He dropped his arms at his side and chuckled. "You don't have to call me *sir*. We're all friends here." He watched her face relax, and she returned the smile.

Fischer stepped up to the small dais and podium in the corner. He had it built two years ago when he took the reins of In-DIGO, and he was the only one who used it. "If we're all finished with the levity," he said, squinting at Kirk and Falstaff. "We shall begin."

He paused for a moment, and Kirk half-expected him to launch into a Gregorian chant or something. Fischer's face looked deadly serious.

"As you all know, we have a mole in InDIGO. Someone with top-level security clearance." He eyed Kirk and Elle, who now sat side by side. "Or possibly someone who had the means to break into our security base." He kept his gaze steady on the pair. "This person or persons has aided in the escape of one suspect as well as played a part in the death of another. We must find them out, and serve them their just desserts."

Kirk noticed that Elle stared straight ahead at the chair in front of her. He couldn't tell if she was deep in thought, or just trying to zone out to keep her temper in check. He knew she didn't care for Fischer, whatever their history had been. Kirk didn't like Fischer much, either. He always did all the right things in the right way. He wore the right clothes and knew the right people. He was too smug. Too snotty.

Kirk slouched down in his chair and listened without allowing Fischer to make eye-contact.

"On top of that, we tried to bring in two of our own agents. Ordered them back to Headquarters. They not only refused outright, but they abandoned millions of dollars worth of top-secret equipment and went rogue in the field." Fischer pointed his nose up and toward Kirk. "We have no way of communicating with them. No way to know if they are somehow in league with Ms. Yakovsky or merely enjoying a bit of European sight-seeing."

Before Kirk realized what she was doing, Elle jumped to her feet. "Don't be a jack-ass, Max. Hedge and Evan would never betray us, and you know it."

Kirk grabbed at her wrist and tried to pull her back to her seat. But the damage was done.

Fischer continued, looking smugger than ever. "Agents Parker and Tyler are not responding to our direct orders." He swept his hand her direction. "Your direct orders, I might add." He placed his hands on either side of the podium and leaned forward with a laser gaze pointed in her direction. "Agent McKinnon, you and Agent Kirk are the best-suited officers in this organization to find Tyler and Parker." He sniffed and leaned back again. "However, you each have prior relationships with them. History that leads me, and others, to believe you would show them deference over InDIGO."

"You!" Elle started to yell, but Kirk took a firm grip on her arm and brought her all the way back to her seat.

"Stop talking now," Kirk muttered. "Don't let him get to you. This is what he wants." He shushed over her when she looked like she was going to start again.

Kirk looked back up toward Fischer. "She's fine, sir. She knows that you're simply doing your job. We all want to get to the bottom of this. We all want to find the mole. As you can see, Agent McKinnon-Grey is quite passionate about it."

Kirk flashed Elle a grimace and let Fischer start again before whispering to her. "He wants to appear tough in front of everyone else. Don't give him a reason to make an example of you. I need you."

Elle released a deep breath. "You need me?"

Kirk stared at her without blinking. He didn't want to tell her what he'd been working on the last two days. He wanted her to have plausible deniability. She was safer in the dark. But not if she was sitting in a cell for insubordination. "*We* need you."

CHAPTER SEVENTEEN

Hedge started to open the door of the maintenance closet, but Evan had an idea and stopped him. "Wait!" she whispered loudly. She put her hand on his arm and squeezed. The light bulb overhead dimmed slightly, and the floor vibrated with a roar of thunder as another train rushed past. Silence followed a few seconds later.

"If someone's out there." She gestured to the door. "They'll be standing on either side of the entry. Probably up against the wall when the train is passing—trying not to get sucked onto the tracks, right?"

Hedge nodded. "Smarty."

She positioned herself precisely in the swing space of the metal door. "I'll wait for the light to flicker again, then I'll pull the door open. You reach out and drag them in, and I'll cover you. Sound good?" She gripped the grimy handle with her left hand, holding her sidearm in her right.

"Sounds perfect." Hedge leaned forward and kissed her forehead. "We're going to make it out of here alive."

Evan rolled her eyes at his sudden confidence. "I know. Were you doubting?"

They both stood ready for several seconds. Hedge looked as anxious as Evan felt. Her stomach fluttered, and she wasn't sure what was causing the butterflies. Today had been crazy. A wedding, a car chase, a foot chase, a subway chase. She'd nearly been torn in half. But then he kissed her.

Stop, girl. You gotta keep your head straight right now. She realized she was holding her breath. She pushed it out over her lips and sipped in another. The train was taking its time.

"How long?" Evan barely finished her question before the bulb blinked. She braced herself and turned the handle.

In one swift motion, she pulled the door open, and a rush of wind roared into the room. In another second a hand with a revolver appeared in the opening. Hedge used his semi-automatic like a hammer, bringing the butt down on his opponent's wrist.

The man fired a shot as Hedge grabbed his arm. Another man, on the opposite side of the door, screamed out in pain. The first man lost control of his weapon, and it skittered across the floor, landing behind Evan. She trained her Springfield on the first man's head as Hedge pulled the second inside. The screamer was clutching at a fresh and very bloody wound just above his knee. Hedge poked his head out for a second and then gave her the all-clear.

Evan closed the door, keeping her aim steady. She kicked the loose revolver out of reach of either man.

Hedge asked them both a question in Ukrainian. Screamer moaned. The other man spat and swore. Evan still didn't know what the word he used meant, but she could guess.

Hedge slapped the man. Screamer started pleading. Evan could see that he thought he was hit in his femoral artery. He wasn't. She'd seen what that looked like. This was a lot of blood, but nothing like arterial spray. Still, if that was what scared him, it was worth a try.

"Your friend is about to bleed out. If you don't answer us, we're going to let him." Evan scowled at both men. She looked up at Hedge when she got nothing but blank stares from the others.

Hedge gestured to the injured man and asked his question again.

This time Potty-mouth responded. Evan guessed that he told Hedge to let his friend die because Screamer howled and lunged at his partner. Hedge pulled him back, dragging him off

Potty-mouth, but not before Screamer buried a blade into his friend's chest. Potty-mouth was silent.

Evan nearly threw up. *Why do they have to do that? Why couldn't they just spill the beans and save themselves?* She looked Hedge in the eye and shook her head. "You got this?" she asked him. "I don't want anyone else dying in here. This closet's too small for all this blood."

Hedge laughed as if she said something funny. She was still trying not to yark.

Screamer moaned again, and Hedge put the muzzle of his pistol to Screamer's temple. "Stupid. Tupyy."

She lowered her body down and picked up the spare revolver. She started to tuck it into her waistband, but then realized she didn't have one. She handed it to Hedge, who slipped it into his. She patted down Potty-mouth and found a cell phone. She turned to Screamer. He looked down at his shirt pocket and pushed his shoulder out slightly. She plucked out his phone and gave both to her partner.

"Somebody's got to get that knife." Hedge gestured to the hilt sticking out of Potty-mouth's sternum. "No weapon left behind."

Evan suppressed her gag reflex. "I'm not pulling it out. You pull it out."

"Don't be a baby." Hedge flicked his empty hand toward Potty-mouth. "Just pull it out. It's not going to hurt him now."

Evan wrinkled her nose. "I'm not a baby. I'll cover this guy. You get the knife."

"I'm the senior officer here. You get the knife."

Evan glared. "I'm your wife. You get the knife." She watched the tell-tale creases forming at the corners of his eyes.

She didn't want to yank a knife out of anyone's chest, but this conversation was working. Screamer was getting scared that he'd lost too much blood, and agitated that he was being ignored.

He yowled and pulled a tiny pistol from his pants pocket. He fired it without aiming, and the bullet stuck in the wall behind them. Evan kneed the side of his head. He dropped the peashooter into Hedge's hand.

Evan knelt down to be eye-level with Screamer. She took a deep breath, knowing what she had to do, as much as it repulsed her. Without blinking, she reached over and pulled the knife from Potty-mouth's chest.

Just don't think about it. Just don't think about it.

Hedge grabbed a handful of the man's hair and pulled his head back at a sharp angle. Evan held the crimson-covered blade to Screamer's cheek. "Who sent you?"

Screamer's eyes went wide. He looked from Evan to Hedge and back.

"Tell us now, and we'll kill you quickly." She pushed the blade flat on his skin.

He looked to Hedge and stuttered, leaning as far from Evan as he could.

Hedge smiled and asked him a question. This time Screamer answered. "Bogdan Klim."

It was a name. She'd never heard the name before, but Evan leaned closer and whispered into the man's ear. "Bogdan Klim?" The smell of urine filled the room. Evan was sure she was going to vomit.

Hedge must have guessed. He jerked Screamer's face away from Evan and toward him. He barked another question as Evan stood again and drew a deep breath. *Nope, now everything smelled like pee.*

"Ni," Screamer answered. "Bogdan Klim lyshe."

Hedge pressed the muzzle of his sidearm above the kneecap of Screamer's other leg. "Costa Alenko?"

Evan held her breath. For every reason.

Screamer looked bewildered. He shook his head. "Ni! Ni! Bogdan Klim. Vyklyuchno." He pleaded.

Hedge relented. Evan exhaled. The light bulb dimmed, and the floor began to rumble.

"Let me clear it." Hedge gestured to the door.

Evan grabbed the handle again and swung the door open. No arms. No heads. Once the train passed, Hedge peeked out in both directions. "We're clear."

Screamer begged.

Hedge shook his head and tossed both of the men's cell phones onto the tracks. "Your friends will find you if they really want to."

Evan stepped out onto the ledge and drew a semi-fresh breath finally. Hedge pulled the door closed when they were out. Evan shrugged. "You're not even gonna lock it?"

Hedge held up the knife. "Don't worry, I'm going to lock it." He pushed the tip into the lock and bent the knife back until the point snapped off. "See?"

Evan nodded her approval. She was exhausted. Her body ached, and she felt coated with dirt, blood, and cold sweat. All she wanted was a shower and a warm place to sleep. As they reached the edge of the main terminal, she hesitated.

"What's wrong?" Hedge asked.

"We can't go back to the flat. We've blown your safehouse. We have nowhere to go."

He took her hand in his and led her to a quiet corner in front of a tile mosaic wall mural. He took off his jacket and handed it to her. She watched him unbutton his dress shirt, which had fewer blood specks than her dress. He gave her his shirt and put his jacket back on over his undershirt. She slipped her arms into the too-big sleeves, and let him roll the cuffs for her.

"I suppose it's good that menswear is a trend for women's fashion." She sighed, looking down and appraising herself. "Can you stand in front of me for just a second?"

He turned away from her and stood guard while she hiked up the side of her skirt and tugged her shredded stockings off. She tapped his shoulder when she was done.

"What did I miss?" He asked, looking her over.

She handed him the wadded ball of nylon. "These are toast."

He took the hosiery and tucked it into his jacket pocket. "We could have used these to tie our friend up. We might need them for someone else later."

Evan followed him up the escalators to the street, her eyes stinging as she stepped out into the sunlight. She scanned every face with every step, straining to see the danger before it could find them. They needed to find shelter, now. They needed time to regroup before they could go after this, Bogdan Klim.

"You got any ideas?"

Hedge shook his head. "Are you sure you don't have any assets in Ukraine?"

She shrugged. "I don't have any assets anywhere." But then a thought jumped into her mind. "Wait. I have a phone number of someone who might help."

"Who is that?" Hedge handed her his phone.

Evan stared at the phone before turning it on. "I'll make one call, then I'll toss it."

"Who are you calling?"

Evan felt her fingers throb as she tapped out the number.

"My friend at MI-6. Mr. Fitzhume."

CHAPTER EIGHTEEN

Hedge and Evan strolled casually to an empty alcove of a storefront. People on the street shuffled past quickly as they hurried home for supper. The sun was dimming. They had no place to go, and it would be dark soon.

Standing in front of Evan, Hedge tried to shield her from anyone who might notice her tattered wedding dress under the men's dress shirt, both with visible blood spatters. Neither wore shoes. While this wouldn't be too unusual in the US, in Kyiv, it was unheard of.

Evan held the phone where they could both hear.

A digital voice said, "You have reached a number that has been disconnected or is no longer in service. Please check the number and try again."

Hedge furrowed his brow. "Are you sure you entered the right number. Country code and all?" Fitzhume had only given Evan his number last week.

"It's the right number." She tilted the phone to study it again. "It's correct. It just doesn't work." She handed the phone back to him.

"You know what that means." Hedge held down the power button until the screen went black. His stomach churned. Even MI-6 was keeping them at arm's length. They had to ditch the phone, and fast. His mind scrambled for the safest place for them to spend the night.

"Is there any chance we can grab something to eat? Do we have any cash left?" Evan's face looked pale.

Hedge weighed the risks. They still had a little cash. The credit card he had in his wallet was as dangerous to use as the phone. The problem was that they needed all the money they had if they wanted to get out of Kyiv without being tracked. But ten bucks wouldn't make a difference. And he was starting to feel a little hollow himself.

"We'll find something fast and cheap." He gestured to the McDonald's at the end of the next block. "We'll splurge. After all, it's our honeymoon." He pulled the credit card out of his wallet and placed the card and the cell phone on the ground in the alcove.

Evan laughed as they pointed themselves toward the golden arches. "You know, I had a lot more energy just a few minutes ago."

Hedge wrapped his arm around her shoulders. "Me too. We'll get some food into us, and maybe it will help our brains to work. Get this all figured out."

They walked the block without making eye contact with other pedestrians. They kept close to the buildings where they could duck in for cover if necessary. Hedge dropped his hand to the center of Evan's back so that he could direct her at a moment's notice.

As they stepped into the intersection with a couple dozen other people, Hedge noticed the crowd in front of them stalling and grumbling as they crossed the street. The hair on his neck stood up, and he gripped more tightly at Evan's waist. "Hold on."

They both halted and watched as the people ahead parted around a man stopped in the center of the road. Andriy.

"You gotta be kidding," Evan muttered.

"Four o'clock." Hedge pulled his Walther from his waistband as they ran back and to the right down the intersecting road. He couldn't see Andriy, but he knew he was close behind them.

Evan ran at full throttle, and Hedge did his best to keep up. His month-old knife wound on his hip was healing and hadn't given him any trouble at all for a week. But right now it was barking at him. He was exhausted. He knew Evan was about done, too.

She turned right again, and Hedge followed her into a dark alleyway. It was barely wide enough for a single small car, and they had to dodge around and jump over discarded boxes and other refuse. Hedge heard a crash behind him. He glanced over his shoulder for just a second to see Andriy had fallen over a bag of trash. He had no intention of slowing.

"Keep going," Hedge urged Evan. She was almost to the end of the alley. A pale wedge of sunlight signaled the next street.

"Keep up," she called back.

Hedge followed her to the left this time. Good. She was moving away from where they had left the cell phone. *She knew what she was doing.*

They ran for another block, away from the safer shopping area and into the more industrialized part of the city. A bus slowed as it passed them, and Hedge had an idea. "On the bus," he yelled.

Evan seemed to speed up and hopped the platform on the side of the bus as soon as it stopped. Hedge was two seconds behind her and ducked just inside the door as the transport started out again. They watched through a window as they passed Andriy, who had apparently not seen them get on.

Andriy scanned the street in both directions and was heading toward the next alley with his pistol raised when they turned the corner and lost sight of him.

Hedge stood close to Evan, and she helped him to conceal his weapon in his jacket pocket. They took the only empty seats about three-quarters back, across from the rear doors.

"Are you okay?" Hedge could hear a rasp in her breathing.

"Yeah. Good." Evan leaned against his arm on the back of the seat. Her hands trembled slightly until she laced her fingers together and dropped them in her lap.

The sky darkened another shade as the bus turned into a maze of factories. The other passengers were headed to night jobs.

Hedge held her for another second and drew a deep breath. He could smell the faded florals of her shampoo and perfumes mixing with the musk of his dress shirt and the sweat from her body.

"We'll get off with them." He barely shifted his finger to indicate the other riders. "Nobody will look for us out here. We'll find a place to sleep. Maybe one of us can dream up an idea to get us out of here."

Evan nodded. "I'm not even hungry anymore." Her stomach growled, betraying her lie.

Hedge snugged her shoulder again. "Me too." He studied the buildings out the windows. Some were lit, others dark. Storage facilities, factories, something that might be a medical clinic. "This is good. Let's go."

They stood and waited for their turn to disembark. Hedge exited first and helped Evan down. He could feel her arm quiver. Maybe it was his. At this point, he just wanted to find a safe place for them to shelter for the night. He'd worry about tomorrow when it came.

They walked by the little clinic. It was lit up within and without. Upon closer inspection, Hedge decided it was probably not a medical building, but a security company. They kept walking. The next block of buildings was a factory, with lights on the first two floors but no sign of life in the top three levels. Getting up there without being stopped could prove a challenge, and he wasn't sure that either of them had the energy to climb stairs.

The next building was a burnt out shell. He didn't want to

deal with that kind of mess. Behind the charred structure was a storage building. The sign on the front was half covered with a black tarp. There were no lights on or in the building. No graffiti outside. No broken windows. It wasn't a Marriott, but he'd slept in worse.

"Let's try this one." He studied the exterior as they approached. No security cameras in sight. He reached for the door handle. It didn't turn. "At least we know the lock works."

"And no alarm." Evan stepped to shield him from view of anyone who might pass. Hedge knelt and pulled his pick set from the hidden pocket in the end of his belt.

"Is it open yet?" Evan shifted her weight from one foot to another, casting a rocking shadow over Hedge's shoulder.

"Not yet. Give me two more seconds." Hedge slid the flat pin into the keyhole and used the notched pin to put pressure on the tumblers in the right order.

"This place has a restroom, probably. Right?" Her dance was becoming more pronounced.

"Probably. We'll just have to look for it." Hedge nodded when the handle turned completely. "After we clear the building."

Evan followed closely behind Hedge as he entered the tiny front room. "I can clear and search at the same time." She had her Springfield drawn before he had the door closed behind them.

The couple searched the room by moonlight. Once that room was secure, they opened the unlocked door straight ahead that led to an open warehouse. This room had no windows, and within seconds they had both stumbled into stacks of boxes.

Hedge rubbed his forehead where it had bumped the corner of a crate. "I'm going to find a light switch if I can. Maybe the building still has power." It took him another full minute to find a wall switch. When he flipped it, he wasn't sure if it went to anything at all. Nothing changed at first. Then he noticed a hint of gray glow spreading from across the room. Several large towers of boxes lined the walls and formed islands throughout the warehouse.

"Do you see a ladies' room sign anywhere?" Evan's tone was urgent.

Hedge turned around him and saw two doors. One was marked with a bolt of lightning, the other with a circle marked WC. "Found it."

He had barely put the period on his sentence when he felt a rush of wind as Evan flew passed him and through the door to the toilet. He heard a faint click and saw a crack of light from under the door. He chuckled when he heard her gasp.

"What on God's green earth is this?" Evan's voice was beyond frustrated. "For Pete's sake," was followed with, "How'm I supposed to... this is not funny. There should be a shower."

Hedge burst into a full belly laugh when she came out, red-faced.

"You knew it would be like that." Evan's hands were clenched at her sides. "Why didn't you warn me?"

Hedge stuffed his laugh and chewed at his lip. "There aren't a lot of Western toilets in this part of the world. Not in warehouses like this."

Evan scowled. "It's a hole in the floor, with footprints on either side."

Hedge nodded. "Affectionately called a squatty-potty."

"Affectionately, I almost fell in."

Hedge laughed again. "The water works?"

Evan rolled her eyes. "Yeah. I'm gonna need back in there in a minute. I'm gonna take a sink bath."

Hedge went into the toilet to relieve himself and to clear his thoughts. Today had been a disaster. Racing across Kyiv on foot, in a car, on a train, and finally a bus. People died. Assets were burned. They had been burned.

They did get a name. Bogdan Klim. Who was he and who did he work for? They'd have to work on that. No more questions for today. He turned the sink tap and an unenthusiastic stream of rusty water splurted into the tiny sink bowl. He cringed at the thought of doing anything but washing his hands with this water.

When he came out of the bathroom, he found Evan trying to read the sides of the boxes. "These big cartons look like car seats. And the smaller ones over here look like umbrella strollers. I'm not sure about anything else."

Hedge nodded. The light had come up enough to make out the crate labels. "You're right. This place sells baby stuff. Go on in and get yourself as cleaned up as possible. That water is iffy, though. Don't drink it or scrub your teeth with it. I'll see if I can scrounge something for us to eat."

Evan sighed. She looked as though she was trying to be angry, but exhaustion was overtaking her.

Hedge went back to the small front room and closed the shades over the two windows flanking the door. He found a double switch and flipped the first one. An exterior light came on and filtered through the curtains. He quickly flipped it back off and tried the other switch. A small desk lamp came on. He made a swift search of the room. An empty desk. A broken chair. A half-size file cabinet. He only found a mini bottle of vodka in the back of a file drawer in the corner. He tucked the bottle into his pocket and turned the lights back off. He double-checked that the outside door was locked, then returned to the warehouse.

Reading the box labels, he found almost nothing useful. High-chairs, mobiles, swings. All baby-sized. He dug deeper. One box of receiving blankets. They might each only be a single yard of fabric, but that was more than they had now. He opened the box.

Behind that was a pallet of something wrapped in plastic. The label only had numbers, no words. He grabbed at the plastic and pulled hard. Once the cellophane was breached, it burst like a can of biscuits. Inside was a dozen crib mattresses. Not ideal, but they would not be sleeping on the concrete floor, anyway.

He went to work arranging a makeshift bed. Evan was still in the water closet, so he continued searching. After another five minutes, he had found a box of teething biscuits and a small carton of baby cereal with applesauce. There were no expiration dates stamped on the containers. He was hungry, and not too proud to try.

He had just finished setting up their dinner on an over-turned crate with a blanket as a tablecloth when Evan returned. She still wore his dress shirt, but the shredded wedding gown was gone. Her hair was twisted into a lovely knot in back. He smiled as he made a grand gesture to the table.

"It's not much, but we won't starve." He sat on the edge of one of the vinyl-covered mattresses and patted the space beside him. "And we'll sleep on actual bedding." He rocked side to side to make the vinyl creak. "It's loud but cushy."

Evan smirked and sat down beside him. She wrinkled her nose at the cereal applesauce combination. "Really?"

He shrugged. "I didn't even find any mashed peas." He held up a curved baby spoon with a bear face on the end. "Our finest silver."

Evan took the spoon from his hand and scooped up a bite of baby food. The expression on her face made Hedge worry that she was going to vomit.

"Please don't lose it." He begged her. "Really. At this point, if you lose it, I may lose it. And I don't have anything in my stomach to toss."

Evan laughed, which was his goal. She picked up one of the teething cookies. "I'll stick with one of these. I don't think I can handle the texture of the mush." She put the cookie into her mouth and pulled it back out almost immediately. "Maybe I'm not hungry."

Hedge nodded and held out the mini vodka. "I found this too, but I can't let you drink on an empty stomach."

Evan bit off half a cookie and grabbed the bottle from his hand. "One cookie, then." She took a gulp of the clear liquid and started coughing.

"Can you breathe?" Hedge asked. "I should have warned you about that, too. Ukrainian vodka is really strong, and it doesn't have any vanilla flavoring. This stuff is why all the men over here only live to be fifty years old."

Evan gasped and then held her side. "It still hurts a little."

Hedge took the bottle from her and set it back on the table. "Sorry. I know you're aching. You wore yourself out today." He got up and turned off the main warehouse light. Now the room was lit only with the glow from beneath the bathroom door.

"I forgot to turn that light off," Evan said.

"No, it's good. We may need it. This room would be pitch black otherwise." Hedge opened the door to the toilet and retrieved her pistol from the side of the sink. "We may need this, too." He closed the door again and returned to the arrangement of mattresses.

He placed her Springfield next to his Walther, between the bed and the table. Taking off his undershirt, he moved to the middle of the mattresses and stretched his legs out, propping himself against the wall. He patted his chest. "Come here, and I'll be your pillow."

Evan scooted to his side and rested her head on his chest, tucking her shoulder into his armpit. "This is nice." She reached her right arm around his waist.

"You know we're sleeping on rubber crib mattresses in

an old warehouse, right?" Hedge took a quick draught from the vodka bottle.

"I know. But we're still alive, and we're still together." Evan took a deep breath and released it slowly. "And the wedding was nice. Even if it wasn't real."

Hedge was trying not to think too much about the wedding. "Yeah," he whispered. "You looked beautiful. You always look beautiful."

Evan snugged her arm around him. "Not right now, I don't." Her voice was growing softer.

Hedge carefully loosened the knot in her hair. Brushing it out over his arm with his fingers. "Even now. Especially now." He continued to brush through her hair, and her body seemed to relax more.

"I, Hedgewick Odysseus Parker," Evan whispered. Her tone was low, and her words ran together. "Take you, Evangeline… ."

Hedge knew she was only moments from sleep. He waited patiently. Her breathing turned into a gentle purr. "I meant every word I said, and then some." He waited a few more minutes, in case she stirred. She didn't. "I love you, Evan."

CHAPTER NINETEEN

The warehouse seemed bigger in the morning. Lighter and almost empty. Warmer. Evan sat at a glass-topped table waiting for her breakfast. She could smell bacon frying nearby. Coffee. Real coffee, too. Her stomach growled. A shiver ran down her spine.

She was still wearing Hedge's dress shirt. Still spattered with blood. She stared through the glass top at her bare feet. Her wine painted toenails still looked pedicure fresh. Everything else on her body was battered and tattered, but her toenails looked amazing.

And she was chewing gum. Stale, fruit flavored, and the piece was too big to chew. Spit it out. She tried to spit it out, but it was stuck—growing inside her mouth. She pulled it out, and it was stuck on her fingers. She couldn't shake it off. And there was still more in her mouth. By the time she finally freed her fingers, the gum in her mouth had grown too big again. It was choking her. She gasped, trying to cry out for Hedge. She pulled on the gum. Not only was it stuck to her fingers, now she couldn't find the end to it. She was strangling.

"Evan, can you hear me?" It was her momma's voice. No, her daddy's.

She tried to answer. The sour gum filled her throat. No air in or out. She kicked her legs, trying to get someone's attention. The white room was dimming to black. She was passing out. She could feel someone clutching her shoulders, shaking her. *Please, just help me get the gum out of my mouth so I can breathe.*

"Evan, I need you to listen to me."

Was it Hedge's voice?

"Wake up. I'm here." That was Hedge's voice.

Her eyes popped open, and she gasped for air. Hedge was holding her in his arms, cradling her head.

"I've got you. It's okay." He whispered. "We need to be extra quiet. I think I heard a car out front."

"Wait!" another voice in her head.

"Wait," she said, holding tight to Hedge's arm.

"I'm not leaving you. I just need to go check it out." Hedge picked up his pistol.

"This is Kirk, Evan. Can you hear me?"

"Yes, I hear you." She squeezed his arm and then pointed to her ear. "It's Kirk."

Hedge froze. "Kirk?"

Evan nodded as Kirk continued. "Let him know I found you. You're in the Happy Baby Merchandise company, right?"

"Yes," she said to both of them. "Kirk found us."

"Okay, listen. I had to do some fancy—never mind. I'll tell you later. Right now, you need to know that I sent you a car. It's parked to the side of your building. It's loaded with everything you need. Clothes, food, paperwork. I've arranged for travel out of Ukraine, too. There are directions to a private airstrip. Tell me where you need to go, and I will let them know when you'll be there and where you're going. The plane will be ready to take off when you get there."

"Red, it's good to hear your voice." Evan nodded to Hedge. "The car is ours. I'll explain in a minute."

Kirk's tone sounded rushed. "Listen, I have to terminate. But I have your back. Don't go to anyone else."

"Wait, Red. We have a name. Can you look it up?" Evan's breathing was starting to normalize.

"Hit me."

"Bogdan Klim."

"You mean Bogdan Klim?" Kirk sounded confused.

Evan sighed. "Yeah. That's exactly what I said."

"The recluse philanthropist that's pushing for Russian-led world climate accords?" Evan could hear Kirk typing as he asked.

She grinned at Hedge. This sounded promising. "Okay, I'm gonna say yes, but just for grins, check out all the Bogdan Klims you might find. A few of his men tried to kill us."

"Will do. And don't forget to tell me where you want the plane to take you."

Evan nodded as if Kirk could see her. "You let us know where Klim is—that's where we want to go."

Hedge took her hand. "Tell him thank you for me."

Kirk didn't wait for her. "You tell Hedge to take care of you."

"I'll tell him." She said to both. "Take care, Red. How do we get in touch with you?"

"You just call me Red, and I'll be here. Just don't take out your earrings."

"And nobody else can track us the way you did?" Evan asked.

"No. I'm using specialized tech that I made specifically for one of my poker buddies. You're safe."

"Love you, Red."

"I know, Evan." And he was gone.

She squeezed Hedge's hand again. "The car outside is for us. Kirk got us everything we need. He's looking up Klim, and he'll have a plane ready for us on demand."

Hedge nodded and stood. "I'll go bring it inside. We need to move soon."

CHAPTER TWENTY

Dressed in a fresh black tee shirt and jeans, Hedge felt seventy-five percent better. A hot shower would top that off, but a shower wasn't available right now. He'd have to make do with the cold sink bath he'd taken. He and Evan had put the warehouse back into decent condition. He set aside some cash for the owner from the stack sent by Kirk.

While Evan was dressing to leave, Hedge checked through all the supplies. It was like Christmas. One envelope contained passports. Passports he knew he could trust. Slipped inside the passports were photo ID cards. Another envelope held cash and credit cards. A small box contained smartphones. One for each of them. They included encrypted emails detailing recent events at InDIGO headquarters. Kirk was the only person on earth he could trust right now.

And Evan.

She came out of the restroom wearing jeans and a gray striped tee. Her hair was tied up in a loose bun on top of her head. She wore her simple diamond stud earrings that sparkled like her eyes. She packed her handbag with the essentials. Lipstick, ID, phone, pistol. And Hedge thought he saw an extra measure of determination go in with everything else.

She was ready to go with a nod of her chin. She was always ready. Hedge marveled at the fact that since the day they met, he hadn't heard her complain about any part of the job. She could have insisted they turn themselves in. She might have suggested they lay low for a while. Instead, she pushed back. Pushed forward.

"Then I guess we're off." Hedge picked up the suitcases and the attache case.

Evan slipped her purse over her head and looped her right arm through the strap. "Do you want to test your earwig now?" She tapped on her earring.

"Is Kirk talking to you?" Hedge asked.

"No, but it will be less awkward if you keep it in your ear than if I have to signal for you to put it in. He may only have a few seconds to communicate with us. It's better to be prepared so we can both hear everything." Evan patted on her bag. "And Kirk says we should have a range up to 100 meters with it."

Hedge smiled and slipped the molded plastic into his ear canal. He turned his face away from Evan and lowered his voice to a whisper. "I got the same message from him."

"Got you loud and clear." Evan tilted her head when Hedge turned back to make eye contact. She reached for her suitcase. "I'll get mine."

"No, I'll get it. You need to heal a little more." Hedge handed her the slim briefcase. "You carry these. All our stuff is probably safer in your hands than mine, anyway."

He gestured toward the door. "Kirk sent a text about Klim. Did you get it?"

"About him being in the Caribbean?"

Hedge held the door open as Evan walked out into the sunlight for the first time that morning. "Yeah. And that he apparently has a home there on Grand Cayman."

Evan helped Hedge load the back seat with their gear. "I think I remember Nastya telling me about an aunt she had who lived in the Caribbean. There could be a connection."

Hedge had been weighing an idea about Bogdan Klim and Costa Alenko since last night. He opened Evan's car door and then closed it when she was comfortably inside the cab. As he rounded the front end of the car, he decided to pitch the idea to her. He got behind the wheel and adjusted the seat. It was worth getting her opinion.

"Do you know what I think the connection might be?" he asked as he pulled away from the Happy Baby warehouse.

Evan turned to him and inhaled a deep breath. "That Alenko and Klim are the same person?" She exhaled as she spoke.

Hedge gripped the leather wheel tightly and turned into a busy roadway. He'd been afraid that he was oversimplifying the situation. It was comforting to know that he wasn't alone in his suspicions. He hadn't been alone in any of this. "Great minds."

Her eyes flashed over a perfect pink smile that told Hedge she offered more than a great mind. He knew. He also knew that though Evan seemed unbothered by their botched mission, behind her glossed smile was an aching heart.

"You know." Evan's voice carried a slight rattle. "When we started this job, it was us against Hrevic. Easy. Then us against Xandra, then Brawn, then Cooper, and now Andriy and Costa... or Klim, or both. Even with all of these targets, it's us against them. But somehow my daddy got mixed in, and I don't know how."

"Evan," Hedge tried to interrupt, but she was unstoppable.

"I don't know which side he's on." She looked away from Hedge, but not before he noticed a shimmer in her eyes. "And our own people are hunting us. I don't know anything anymore."

"Evan." Hedge sharpened his tone. He needed her to focus. He needed her to stay sharp. "Evan, you do know. You do."

"What do I know?"

"You know your father." He paused a moment to let her nod. He reached out and patted her hand. "You know him. You know that he would never do anything to hurt you."

She inhaled and ran the side of her finger under her bottom lashes. "I know that." She exhaled. "But why did he kill a man in broad daylight? The man we were supposed to meet?"

Hedge chuckled. "Broad daylight makes a difference?" He shook his head. *Don't tease her; she's upset.* "I know this is a mess. But when we find your father, he'll tell us what's happening. Right?"

She raised her palms upward in surrender. "Last week I thought he was a consultant for an oil company. Do you think he'll tell us the truth about anything?"

Hedge read the road sign indicating that the airstrip was just ahead. "Almost there." He turned his face away from her. "Com check," he whispered.

"Good to go."

Turning the car off the main road and onto the narrow drive of the small airport, Hedge sniffed and shrugged. "You may be right. Your father lied to you in London. Lied to your mother. Who knows what he would say if you confronted him?"

Evan spun to face him, her face was red and blotchy. "Don't talk like that about my daddy. He is a good man!"

Hedge leaned his shoulder away from her. His accusation had worked. "I know that, and you know that. I just wanted you to say it. You needed to remind yourself. Sometimes you have to do that out loud."

Evan rocked her head back against the seat. "Why did he lie to me?"

A shuttle van was parked under the canopy at the side of the hangar. Hedge gestured to the small jet at the end of the runway. "That's our ride." He parked next to the van and killed the engine. "You lie to your mother about what you do. Why?"

"To protect her, of course. And to keep her from worrying." Evan slipped her purse strap over her shoulder. She handed the paperwork to Hedge. "I know you're trying to help."

"But?"

"It's working." She sounded disgusted.

A young man wearing a gray jumpsuit, an orange vest, and headphones around his neck tapped on the driver-side window.

Hedge lowered the glass. "Making a beer run," he said.

The young man nodded. "Cerveza?"

Correct response. Hedge pointed to the back seat, and the man extracted the suitcases. As jumpsuit carried the bags to the plane, Hedge turned to face Evan. "We can talk more on the plane. It's going to be okay." He looked at the shuttle just beyond her door. "Did I park too close?"

Evan flashed her smile again. "No, I'm good." She pulled on the door handle and paused. "Next stop, Grand Cayman."

They both got out of the sedan and started toward the tarmac. Before they rounded the front of their car. A man stepped out of the passage door to the hangar. Andriy.

Hedge tossed the envelope of papers back to Evan and reached for his pistol. Andriy charged him before he could raise the muzzle. Hedge swung his elbow up and into Andriy's jaw, sending him back and into the hangar wall. Raising his Walther, he waved for Evan to keep her distance.

"Zalyshtes'!" Hedge yelled. "Stay back." He kept his pistol trained on Andriy's head.

Andriy smiled and raised his revolver toward Evan. Hedge didn't hesitate. Firing two quick shots, he dropped Andriy where he stood.

Letting his shoulders fall, Hedge turned to face Evan. Before he could say a word, the shuttle van behind her moved forward. The side door slid open, and a man in a black hood reached out and pulled her inside. The van squealed away, leaving only the envelope of papers on the ground.

"Evan!" Hedge barked. He tried to shoot out the van tires, but his bullets glanced off the paving. "Evan, can you hear me?"

"Yes." A whisper in his ear.

"We don't have much time." He grabbed the papers and jumped back into the car. "Keep talking, and I'll find you."

"You have to go. Leave me here, and I'll find you. Or you'll find me. Just go and catch Klim." Evan's voice was quiet, with a roar behind it. "Go."

"I promised you I would never leave you. I can't." He turned the car in the direction of the van, but he couldn't see the other vehicle anywhere. "I won't leave you."

"You have to go. You may lose the only chance we have." She gasped. "I trust you to find me. Now you have to trust me to take care of myself. Get on that plane." Her voice crackled in his ear.

"I'm not leaving you. I'm just a minute or two behind you." He swerved when he saw what looked like the van sitting a few meters off the road behind some bushes. He hopped from his car and approached cautiously, weapon drawn. As he rounded the back of the shuttle, he saw the side door was open. He inched up, ready for anything. Except what he found.

The vehicle was empty. Everyone was gone. On the edge of the seat lay a pair of diamond stud earrings. His last connection to Evan.

Hedge circled the van, looking for clues. No clear tracks or footprints in the leafy ground. He walked back to his car and stared out at the vacant road. She was gone.

He drove back to the hangar and looked up at the plane. He didn't want to leave her, but he couldn't afford to lose Klim, either. "I will find you, Evan."

CHAPTER TWENTY-ONE

Kirk sat up and looked around his dark bedroom. His laptop speaker was humming, and his desk lamp was flashing. He turned to look at his clock. A quarter past three in the morning. He'd been asleep for two hours.

He'd set several alarms for Hedge and Evan. One to sound if either of their names appeared in an InDIGO memo. One for if Evan's receiver was turned off. One for if the trackers on their phones were more than 100 meters apart. And of course, one to sound if either of them were messaging or calling him.

As he staggered from his double bed to his glass-topped desk, he wondered if he was conscious enough to be of help to anyone. He flipped open the notebook computer and brought up his alarm applications. This stopped the flashing of the lamp.

"Gloria, work mode," he commanded into the darkness. The lamp turned back on, the thermostat glowed blue as the room temperature reset, and the small coffee pot on the dresser started brewing.

Kirk's computer screen showed multiple alarms, in the reverse order in which they were triggered. They were too far apart —moving in opposite directions, actually. And her receiver was off.

"Well, crap!"

Just as he was downloading GPS coordinates for Evan's phone, another alarm popped up. Hedge was calling.

"What is going on there? Why are you separated?" Kirk didn't bother saying hello. He was awake now, and mad.

Hedge sounded just as angry. "She was taken. We were about to get on the plane. We were ambushed. A man tried to kill us; I got him. But then a couple more grabbed her and sped away. I could communicate with her for a minute, but then nothing."

Kirk tapped away on his keys, looking for something. "And you just let her go?"

"No. I followed as fast as I could, but they switched vehicles. I didn't know who or what I was chasing."

Kirk growled. "And you gave up and left her behind? You're on the plane, heading over the Atlantic." How could Hedge leave Evan behind? It was his job to protect her. *Should've never left her side.*

"We were followed. Tracked somehow." Hedge's voice returned the accusation. "You assured us that wouldn't happen. Couldn't happen."

Shaking his head as if Hedge could see him, Kirk said, "The docs and gear I sent were clean. The car, too. You got sloppy."

"We were careful. These people were waiting there for us. You had to have leaked our location to someone."

"I'd never do that." Kirk added, "I wasn't hacked either."

"How can you be so sure?" Hedge asked.

"Why are you so sure it was me?"

"They took out her earrings. It was someone who knew about her receiver implant. That narrows it down to just a handful at InDIGO." Hedge's voice sounded strained. "Kirk, we trusted you."

"Shut up, Hedge. You still do." He continued scouring his information. "Or you wouldn't have gotten onto the plane."

Kirk expected another accusation or harsh comeback but got nothing. Another second of silence and he heard Hedge sighing.

"There's one other person who knows that Evan has a receiver in her ear canal." Hedge's tone turned somber. "Xandra knows."

"And her trail has gone cold. Nothing since she escaped custody." Kirk pulled up another program running in the background. "I've had facial rec alarms set for her since the morning I heard she was in the wind. But nothing."

"I don't doubt you, or your skills. I just have to know something." There was exhaustion in Hedge's voice. "How can you be so sure that nobody tracked us?"

"I used unique encryption that only activates with a particular phone app that I created. Less than a dozen people have the app installed, and I know and trust every single one."

"And who are the others?"

Kirk swallowed hard. Confidentiality was his hallmark. He couldn't break a trust. "I can only say that the others are members of my poker group."

"And it's impossible for one of them to be involved?" Hedge's accusations were becoming snippy. Kirk knew he was growing impatient.

Just as Kirk was about to answer, another alarm popped up on his screen. "Hedge, I just got a high-alert notification that you and Evan are responsible for the death of another InDIGO agent in Kyiv. Andriy Popovic. Do you know anything about this?"

A heavy sigh. "Yeah. I shot Andriy this morning. He was about to kill Evan. Didn't think he was InDIGO. I thought he worked for Klim. I suppose nothing really surprises me, though. Does it say who was with him? That's who took her?"

"Nothing." Kirk sighed. "Look, her cell just came back on. It looks like she's stopped at the side of the road. Call her phone and see if anyone answers. I tried through my computer but got no answer. You keep trying. I'm going to intensify the search for Xandra."

"Got it." Hedge didn't disconnect immediately. "Kirk?"

Kirk rubbed his eyes as he leaned in to read the next notification on his screen. "I know, Hedge. But she can take care of herself." He had to say it out loud to remind himself.

"I know, but—"

"If I hear anything, no matter how small, I'll let you know. And you do the same. After all, she was my girl before she was yours."

"I know. I will."

CHAPTER TWENTY-TWO

Before she realized she was being taken, Evan felt a sharp prick in the bend of her elbow. She fought the hand that grabbed and held tight. A chill raced up her arm, and soon her whole body wrestled in slow motion. Her hands were jelly, unable to ball into a fist. She couldn't kick straight. She was a flailing fish, and soon not even that.

She didn't lose consciousness this time. The last time she'd been taken, it was with a conk on her noggin that gave her a concussion. She was grateful to still be aware. Her mind was sharp, but her body was useless.

She could hear Hedge's voice in her receiver. Evan told him to go on without her. He'd find her later. Find Klim. Why did she tell him to leave her? All she wanted was Hedge at her side. Why would she send him away?

In the van, she glimpsed two men with black masks. One of them dropped a hood over her head. They didn't bind her. They didn't have to. She couldn't move. They held her upright on the bench seat. One of the men raised her hood halfway. He pushed her hair to one side and removed her left earring. Then her right. They knew about her ear canal implant. InDIGO.

She couldn't fight, not with her body. But she would think and talk. The question was what to say.

The black bag over her head smelled like fresh laundry. It smelled better than she did. *Thanks for that.* The road changed from fairly smooth to jostle-your-fillings bumpy. The van stopped.

Bad things happen when the vehicles stop.

Evan held her breath as she heard the side door slide open.

The men didn't speak. This was all planned ahead. She felt an arm slip under her knees and another around her back. She was lifted out of the van and carried to another automobile. The second one was slightly higher than the van, she believed.

She focused. She knew she needed to remember everything.

She inhaled deeply as the man set her into the seat. His scent seemed familiar. Cedar, tobacco, cherries. Cigars. She tried to think. Doors opened. Doors closed. An engine sputtered and then purred. They were moving again.

Unsmoked cigars. *It couldn't be. He wouldn't.*

"Daddy?"

The hood was pulled off. There were two men, unmasked, up front, and next to her sat her dad.

"Hey, Punkin' Pie." As if he had just picked her up from ballet lessons.

"What on earth are you doing? Have you lost your everlovin' mind?"

"I know this looks bad." This time his voice was conciliatory.

"You kidnapped me. You took me from Hedge. He needs me." Evan's blood was boiling now. She thought she might be getting some muscle control back in her fingers. "You can't just haul off and kidnap me!"

"I told you she'd be angry." It was the driver. She recognized his voice, too.

"Uncle Clint?" Evan stared at the back of Clint's balding head for a second before shifting to look into the rear-view mirror into his smiling eyes.

She quickly turned to see that the other man in the front seat was Cole Waxman, her dad's fishing buddy and business associate. And apparently much more. "Mr. Waxman?"

Evan finally could move enough to shift her body to face her dad. "You drugged me. You shanghaied me from my job. You dragged your friends into something where y'all could all be killed." She lowered her voice to a whisper. "Not to mention you killed a man I was supposed to meet."

"Listen to me," Gordon Tyler took his fatherly tone. "That man I shot was sent to kill you and Hedge. I saved your life."

Making a fist and releasing it, Evan chuffed. "And the man you were with then? He did shoot me. My ribs are still bruised."

"I know. Now." Gordon nodded. "You check people out as best you can. But people lie."

Evan's jaw dropped. "Oh! If you're not the pot callin' the kettle."

Gordon laughed, hugging her shoulders. "I sure have missed you, Ev."

The car stopped at a gas station on a hill overlooking the river and the whole city of Kyiv. On the top of the opposing bank, Evan could see the Motherland sculpture stretching up to the clouds.

"Can I get out and try to walk for a second?" Evan could shift her legs but wasn't sure if they had the strength to carry her.

"Yeah, just don't run, okay?"

Evan waited until her dad could help her out. They stood side by side for several seconds, looking at the statue of the giant silver woman piercing the sky with a sword in her right hand and a broad shield in her left.

"Over sixty meters to the top," Gordon said.

"Daddy, you have to take me back. Hedge needs me." Evan pointed to the monument. "I'm a lot like her, you know?"

"Really tall?"

"Ready for a fight." She faced him again. "Please don't make me fight you."

"I just want to protect you." Gordon shoved his hands into his pockets.

"I know. But I have a job to do."

Gordon reached out to smooth a stray curl on Evan's head. "That's the thing. Your job is over. The people who gave you this job are trying to kill you."

"First off," Evan said as she planted her hands on her hips. "I know that, and I'm working very hard to keep myself and my partner alive. Second, don't you think if they're trying to kill us, that there's still quite a bit of work needin' to be done?"

"Gah, you're just like your mother." Gordon shook his head. "Okay, so what's the third thing.?"

Evan's eyes teared. *Uggh. Just talk to him without getting emotional.* "Third, well, I had something, but now I can't remember it. You got me all flustered talkin' about Momma."

"Just like her." Gordon pulled Evan into a hug as Clint and Mr. Waxman got back into the car. "What do you need, baby girl?"

"I need my earrings back so I can talk to Hedge."

They got into the car again.

Gordon tapped Waxman on the shoulder. "Do you have her earrings?"

He shook his head. "I left them in the van."

Drawing a controlled breath through her nose and releasing it through her mouth, Evan squared her shoulders. "I need to speak with Hedge. He's on his way to find a very dangerous man, and he needs to know that I'm alright. AND that I'm on my way with help."

"He's looking for Bogdan Klim?" Gordon asked.

"Yes, we believe he's really Costa Alenko. We know he's not the top of the pyramid, but he's gotta be close to the top. Everyone else is dead now."

Gordon pushed his lips in and out. Evan knew this mean he was thinking. Holding a spirited debate in his mind. "And you believe Klim is in the Caribbean?"

"We have reason." Evan kept her words short. This was the best way to get her dad on her side.

He reached behind him on the seat and pulled out her purse. "Your phone is probably in here."

Evan snatched up her handbag and shuffled through it for her phone. "Thank you, Daddy."

Gordon reached out and took her hand, wrapping her phone within her fingers. "Why are you not asking me whose side I'm on? Who I'm working for?"

Evan stared into her father's eyes. "Because I trust you, Daddy."

CHAPTER TWENTY-THREE

The phone powered up and the screen showed four missed calls with coordinating voicemails and six texts. Evan didn't bother reading or listening to any of the messages. She punched the name *Hedge* and listened for the line to connect.

"Can you put it on speaker?" Gordon asked.

"No." She listened for half a second more.

"Evan, are you all right?" He sounded strained.

"I'm fine. Are you on your way to Grand Cayman?" Relief surged through her at the sound of Hedge's voice.

"I should have never left you. How did you escape?" He paused. "I'll have the pilot turn around."

"No." Evan turned her face from her dad and the others. She lowered her tone. "Don't come back for me. I'll come to you right away. I didn't exactly escape. I didn't have to."

Evan could hear the urgency in Hedge's voice. "Make sure you hide any bodies well. InDIGO has a high alert for both of us now since I killed Andriy."

"No bodies to hide." Evan tried to think of a good way to explain. "I know the people who took me. They won't hurt me."

"What do you mean? You know them? Evan, you can't trust anyone." Evan thought she heard Hedge swear, and she was glad she didn't have the speaker on. Hedge's voice grew louder. "How can you get a flight out? Have you spoken to Kirk already?"

Evan took a deep breath. "I can get a flight. We're arranging that now. We won't use the same airstrip."

"You keep saying *we*."

"Yeah, I found my dad."

This time Hedge roared through a dozen curses before taking a breath. "Your father is the one who kidnapped you?"

Evan's heart pounded. She knew Hedge wasn't angry with her, but she didn't like hearing his temper flare. "Yeah. He thought he was protecting me."

"From me?" Hedge was loud enough that everyone could hear him without the speaker.

"No."

Gordon leaned over Evan's shoulder. "Yes. From anyone who might put her in danger."

Evan pushed him back and cradled her phone closer to her ear. "He doesn't mean that." Evan could hear Waxman calling for a flight. He used code when speaking, and it reminded him of when Kirk had made arrangements for them. "Hedge, hang on a sec." She shifted toward Waxman. "Where did you learn that code?"

Mr. Waxman turned to face her. "From a friend."

"From whom?" She fixed her face with her most serious expression. Waxman blinked.

"From one of my poker buddies."

Evan's eyes crossed. "Oh, for Pete's sake. Hedge, did you hear that?"

"I can't hear anything. Put it on speaker." He said it like it was an order.

Evan drew a deep breath. "Okay, everyone. I'm turning on the speaker. Y'all all jus' behave."

Hedge's voice was considerably louder through the speaker, though his tone seemed to calm. "What was I supposed to hear?"

Evan turned to Gordon. "Daddy, are y'all three the infamous poker buddies we hear so much about?"

Gordon stammered. "Well, yes, but— "

"But nothin.' Red thinks y'all are some sort of Illuminati or something. He's making mission plans based on your advice." Evan rubbed her temples. "It's a wonder we haven't blown up all of Europe."

"Evan," Hedge's voice interrupted. "Hang on."

She didn't stop. "You three guys are playing some game that you know nothing about. Poker buddies, fishing buddies, hunting buddies. Do you understand the damage you could have caused?"

Hedge's voice boomed over the speaker. "Evan!"

Her mouth snapped closed. Gordon swallowed loud enough to get her attention.

"Agent Parker," Gordon spoke in measured paces. "Are you aware of our organization?"

"Yessir. I am aware." Hedge sounded professional again. "What service may I provide, sir?"

Evan gasped. Now Hedge was falling in. Why? This was her daddy and uncle. And Mr. Waxman, for Pete's sake.

"Well, to begin with, you can educate my daughter about us. I thought Kirk had taken care of that, but apparently not." Gordon's tone was icy. He shot a reprimanding glance at Evan. "I suppose that can wait 'til later. For now, when you get to the island, please arrange for accommodations for Evan, yourself, and me. Waxman and Clint will be going on to another location to follow up a second lead on Klim. I'll notify Kirk to run ID traces on anyone arriving or departing Grand Cayman for the next five days."

"Sir." Hedge paused only for a second. "Sir, my pilot has notified me that I'll probably be losing cell service in the next five minutes. May I speak to Evan again privately?"

"Sure." Gordon tapped the speaker button and gently

moved the phone back to Evan's slacked jaw.

"What just happened?" she asked. "Is my daddy your boss?" She stared at the three men in the car with her for a second, then closed her eyes, imagining Hedge's face.

"We'll talk about that tonight. I just need to know that you're really okay."

"Hedge, I really am. I just wish we were together right now. This is all too bizarre." She felt like a teenager. "Are you okay?"

"Yeah. I shouldn't have left you. I swore I wouldn't."

"Shh." Evan tried to turn in a way to keep her conversation private. "We only have a minute."

"I want to talk to you about something important when you get here. So try to rest on your flight. Text when you get close. I'll be waiting for you when you touch down."

As Evan listened to Hedge talk, she could feel her eyes stinging. "I can't wait. I have something I need to tell you, too."

Hedge chuffed, and Evan could almost feel his breath in her ear. "You don't have to wait. You can go ahead and tell me."

Heat bubbled from Evan's belly, like the sensation of drinking too much red wine. Her face flushed hot and her fingertips throbbed. She'd wanted to tell him how she felt for a long time. Could she say it now, over the phone, with her dad eavesdropping?

She drew a deep breath. "I love you, Hedge," she whispered.

He didn't answer. *Oh, dear lord, too much. Too soon.* "Hedge?" She waited another three seconds. Still nothing. She looked at her phone.

Call failed. Disconnected.

She felt her chest tighten. Did he hear her? Evan's ears

began ringing. She dropped the cell into her bag and dropped her head into her hands. Uggh. Why was everything a struggle with Hedge? No, not with Hedge; with her.

She felt a warm hand on the center of her back. "Don't worry, baby girl. He knows."

Gordon pulled her into a hug. Evan pushed her face into his shoulder, hoping any stray tears would mop off. She needed to be tough. This was a big deal for her, and she messed it up. And the last thing she wanted to do was get a lecture from her dad. She decided to turn the tables.

She sat up and turned to face her dad squarely. "Are you guys really Illuminati?"

CHAPTER TWENTY-FOUR

Hedge couldn't wipe the smile from his face no matter how he tried. He'd dragged their bags and paperwork from the tiny runway in the grass to the Uber he had arranged. At the beach-side resort, he was able to get two small suites that were not adjacent, but on the same wing.

He unpacked their bags and took a fast shower. He ran the water much warmer than he typically would. The heat worked to loosen his stiff neck and shoulders. Unlike the narrow plastic shower stalls in Ukraine, this glass shower had room for two. The rest of the bathroom was tiled in polished slate, with a glossy white sink cabinet and a six-foot egg tub. At the end of the room was a glass wall looking out over the beach with teal blue water beyond. Like her eyes.

All he could think about was Evan.

He dressed in a navy golf shirt and khakis. The concierge helped him rent an SUV which would be delivered in thirty minutes. Time to scout the place.

Hedge ambled down from the third floor and out to the pool area. The pool was a cool blue-green rectangle, with semi-circles cut from the sides and corners, punctuated with palm trees. Red lounge chairs lined the perimeter, and white and gray umbrellas stood ready for shade. The whole scene sat in the shelter of the white stone, L-shaped, ten-story modern stacked hotel.

A paved walk and a short seawall broke the stretch of property between the lush green landscaping and the white sand beach. Hedge walked and watched. Scanning faces. Looking for whatever might draw Klim to the island. At the farthest point of the beach, he pulled out his digital binoculars and skimmed the residences on either side of the resort.

Most of the homes were shrouded in palms. Only colorful tiled rooftops pierced through the greenery. Plenty of privacy.

He walked back to the hotel and picked up his vehicle, ready to meet Evan and Gordon. The sun was dipping low toward the water, painting the sky with red and orange slashes.

As he drove back to the grassy landing strip, he passed several banks and offices closing their doors for the night, while the restaurants and nightclubs turned on their neon beacons.

He wished Evan was there. She would see it, whatever it was. He needed her eyes. He needed her. The smile was back.

She would be here soon. She'd be tired. He'd let her sleep. For a little while.

CHAPTER TWENTY-FIVE

Evan tried to get comfortable in the narrow charter plane seat as she scrolled through the article on her phone. Bogdan Klim was reclusive, that was simple enough. No known photos of the man, only a few descriptions from people who didn't seem to think much of him.

She tried to pull her foot up underneath her, but the length of her shin bone exceeded the breadth of the seat cushion. Instead, she turned sideways and hung her legs over the armrest and into the aisle. She checked the time. Still another twenty minutes before they'd land. She glanced out at the balance of sky above and water below for as far as she could see.

She had only been able to sleep for a few hours. And the dreams kept that from being restful. She felt better working, anyway. No good to worry about what Hedge heard or didn't hear. Focus on the mission.

She adjusted her eyes back on the screen. It just didn't make much sense. In one situation Kilm was described as being in his mid-to-late fifties with dark hair, hooded gray eyes, and a low, sharp voice. Next as mid-thirties, sparkling green eyes with sandy hair and a light, cheerful accent. That sounded more like Michael Cooper. But both stated he was shorter—less than six feet tall, and nobody would ever suggest that Cooper was anything under six-two.

Disguises can change eye or hair color, but you can't make yourself shorter. So Cooper wasn't Klim. Was it Costa Alenko? Or someone else?

No record of him until eleven years ago. Even that was slim information. He donated a substantial amount of money to an environmental organization studying the impact of offshore drilling. Another mention of Klim as part of an investment firm in northern Africa. In Russia. In China. Most recently in Spain.

But no pictures.

Most philanthropists wanted publicity. If not for themselves, for the organizations they supported. If being in front of a camera had taught her anything, it was that people wanted to know more. If she carried the right handbag in a magazine photo, it would sell out the next week. Celebrity might be fleeting, but for that flash of a moment, a star—for better or worse—mattered, and whatever they said, wore, praised, supported, or even attacked made a difference.

Why hide?

Barring physical deformity, which indeed would have been mentioned in any reference, Evan couldn't think of a reason, unless he was in hiding. In an age when there are literally tens of thousands of cameras per square mile, why was there not a single snapshot of this man?

She thought about his investment firm. What was the name? She scrolled back up. Ves' Mir Investments.

"Daddy, what does Ves' Mir mean?" She straightened herself in her seat as her dad turned to face her from the row ahead.

"It's Russian. It means the whole world. What are you reading?" Gordon scrunched his eyebrows low over his eyes.

"Jus' doing a little research on Klim. His investment company is called Ves' Mir." She handed her phone to her dad. "Everything comes back to energy and natural resources."

Gordon nodded, handing the phone back. "The world's only true currency."

Evan laughed. "Yeah. Which one of your poker buddies told us we needed to invest in gold? Kirk mentioned there was a push for the International Monetary Fund to make a move away from the US dollar as the fiat currency and shift to the gold standard."

Cole Waxman raised his finger. "That's what I discovered. Not through verified or official channels, but there is a quiet push underway."

The overhead belt light dinged on, and without a word, everyone fastened their lap strap. Evan leaned forward so that Gordon and Waxman could hear her over the sound of the engine noises as the plane prepared to land. "Who benefits from the gold standard? Doesn't the US have as many natural resources as most places in the world?"

Waxman sighed. "Not in reserve. Technically, we have plenty within the borders. But not everything on American soil is available to the government. Same with every country, but where other governments just take whatever they want from private citizens, our government has laws against that."

"And rightly so," Gordon added.

"Gold reserves in Fort Knox, for example." Waxman turned enough to set his face in profile for Evan. "If the American dollar is fiat, and China calls all their loans due, the mint can create a tiny gold coin that says it has a value of ten trillion dollars. Easy. They wouldn't, but they could if pushed. On the other hand, if gold was fiat, and China calls the loans due, we go bankrupt. We don't have the gold reserves on hand. Nobody does."

"So we need to be looking in China?" Evan exhaled a dramatic sigh.

"No, the country doesn't matter. It's the same with Russia, or wherever. That's why we trade more than gold. We have oil, gas, coal, copper, silver, and platinum. Even diamonds and other gemstones. Technology, too."

Evan's head was spinning. Too much information. If the wrong person was in control, very bad things could happen. "We have plenty of oil. Some geologists say that we have more untapped reserves than active—oh why am I telling you this. You know."

"We do." Gordon nodded. "But there are plenty of people trying to shut down production in the US for environmental reasons."

Evan patted her phone. "Yeah. It said Klim supported an environmental research group. But that's not a bad thing."

"Not at all. So long as we value the lives of humans over money. But some people will make a report say anything that benefits their pocket. And that's on both sides of the argument." Gordon gripped his armrest as the landing gear clunked into position.

Evan rocked her head back against the seat and wished Hedge was beside her. She knew she'd see him soon, but his warm hand would feel reassuring right about now.

Another thought popped into her mind. "How do you find out who controls the resources? The reports? The money?"

"The companies who pump the oil and mine the gold have a little control. They produce what they can sell at their desired price. Supply and demand. There are some other factors, of course, but mostly the companies." Waxman turned back to face forward.

"And who is in charge of the companies. Like Vis' Mir, how do we find that out?" Evan focused like a laser.

"More research," Gordon said. His grip tightened on the armrest.

Evan smiled at the realization that her dad didn't like flying. It surprised her. She swallowed hard, and her ears popped with the change in cabin pressure. A sudden crackle in her ear quickened her heartbeat. "Hedge?" she whispered.

"Kirk."

A smile broke across her face. She was about to shout until he stopped her.

"Don't say anything. I'm only talking to you now because I can scramble my transmission easier while you're landing. I've been listening to your conversation. I think you have something. I've spent the last 72 hours scouring the planet for Xandra and couldn't find her anywhere. But then I did a little checking on Ves' Mir Investments. Long-story-short, and without hacking into bank records, which is highly illegal, even for me, I found an appointment for a meeting with a Ves' Mir officer at a Grand Cayman bank. Tomorrow at eleven o'clock local time."

Evan drew a deep breath.

"Stop. I mean it. Do not speak. It's not Klim. The meeting is with Anastacia Alenko. Nastya. And the appointment was made two days ago. I'll send Hedge the details. Be careful." And then Kirk's voice disappeared into another crackle.

Evan stared at the back of the seat in front of her. In ten minutes she and her dad would be on Grand Cayman Island. With Hedge. And probably Bogdan Klim, whoever he was. And with someone pretending to be Nastya. That could only be one person.

Xandra.

CHAPTER TWENTY-SIX

Evan hadn't realized how chilled she was until she stepped out into the humid Caribbean air. She followed her dad down the airstair to the tarmac. Waxman and Clint came after her, but only to pick up snacks in the hangar while the plane refueled. They were heading out immediately after.

Evan scanned the grassy strip. A charcoal SUV approached and stopped at the edge of the paving. Hedge stepped out and saluted. She wanted to run to him. Before she could decide on her next move, she saw her dad making quick strides toward him. Now she had to hurry to keep up.

"Sir." Hedge offered his hand to Gordon. "It's a pleasure to finally meet you."

Evan watched Hedge's face. He looked every bit as nervous as her very first date, standing on their front porch. Gordon shook his hand and dipped his chin. "Parker," was all he said.

Evan reached out for a hug, but Hedge grabbed her hand and shook it as well. "Agent Tyler. Glad you're back in one piece."

Crap! He heard. And it was too much. She should never have said the L-word. Uggh. He'd go right back to professional. She couldn't deal with this right now. There was too much to do. She took a deep breath. "Did you get some info from Kilo?" She could do professional. For the moment.

"Got it." He said, gesturing toward the vehicle. "Mr. Tyler, won't you sit up front with me? Evan won't mind the back seat."

"Thank you, Parker. I appreciate that."

The back seat? Evan climbed in behind her dad without help and slammed the door. She scowled for a second while her eyes adjusted to the black interior and black tinted windows.

On the seat next to her sat Hedge's phone, opened to a messaging app. She picked it up and read.

Kirk had sent everything. A bank contact at the Queen's Bank of Cayman, along with the contact's agenda. Ms. Carol Freemont will be meeting Anastacia Alenko tomorrow at eleven. The note on the schedule was that Ms. Alenko would bring sufficient identification to facilitate a withdrawal as well as a transfer of funds to a new account. There was also a phone number for Alenko, which Kirk noted was a dummy set up with a voicemail recording.

She looked up at Hedge and nodded. Like her, he was unsure about when or if to let her dad in on all the plans. Kirk wanted everything quiet. That was yet another thing to discuss when they got to the hotel.

"You say you got two suites?" Gordon asked. "That will be fine."

Evan almost didn't care. After sleeping on a fold-out sofa bed, a plastic crib mattress, and then in an airplane seat, anything would feel like a suite to her.

She looked out the dark windows at the road lined with palm trees and the orange-purple sky overhead. Inside the car, she could smell the water. Clean. Salt. Her stomach growled. She wanted to eat. She wanted to sleep. But she needed to talk with Hedge.

The road from the airport twisted through Georgetown and up toward the West Bay area. Hedge seemed to slow the car as they passed the Queen's Bank. Beyond that, she saw a sign for the public beach and then a tall modern building appeared on her left.

She felt a slight flutter when Hedge turned into the adjacent parking lot.

"Home," he announced. He shot her a glance in the rearview mirror, and Evan thought she saw a spark in his eye.

Was that good or bad?

The valet greeted them, and Gordon took his duffle from the SUV. Hedge handed over the keys to the young man and nodded, slipping him a handful of cash.

The valet smiled and nodded back. "Thank you, sir."

Hedge led them through the lobby and to the elevator. They allowed an older couple to exit before they got in the carriage.

Gordon broke the quiet. "Two suites? Are we on the same floor?"

Hedge nodded. "Yes, sir. Across the hall and two doors down."

The elevator arrived at three, and the doors slid open. The hall was empty, and Hedge directed them to the right. "Just down here." He handed Gordon his room key.

"Great. Thank you, Parker." He smiled at Evan.

Her heart was pounding. She was holding her breath.

Hedge offered his hand again, and Gordon shook it.

"I guess we'll get cleaned up and dressed for dinner." She couldn't think of anything else to say.

Gordon chuffed. "Parker, are you already unpacked?"

"Yes. When I got here."

"Good. You can bring my daughter's bag to my room, and we'll let you know when we're ready to eat."

Evan blinked. *What?* She started to say something but stopped mid-breath.

"Sir," Hedge began. "Evan is in my room. Our cover is that we're married."

Gordon cocked his head to one side. Evan knew that meant he was pretending not to understand what he heard. "No, that was your cover in Kyiv. We're not in Kyiv anymore. I just arrived with my daughter. That's my cover."

Evan watched with wide eyes. Hedge clinched his fists and drew a deep breath. Her dad leaned forward a fraction of an inch. *This was not good.*

"I think...." She didn't even get the third word in.

"Mr. Tyler, I understand that you miss your daughter. That you love her."

Gordon shook his head. "No, Parker. You have no idea how much I cherish my daughter."

He used the word *cherish*. That's what he'd told every boy that ever dated her.

"Sir, you're right. I can't fully know that." Hedge loosened his fists. "But I made a promise to her that I would never leave her side."

"And then you did just that. Twenty-four hours later you left her. You got on a plane and abandoned her." Gordon inched his foot between Evan and Hedge.

"You kidnapped her!"

Evan knew that Hedge was struggling to keep his voice low. She could also see the glazed look in his eyes. Her dad wasn't doing much better.

"I kidnapped her to protect her."

"I didn't...." Evan couldn't get a word in edgewise.

Hedge made a low growl and sucked in a deep breath before continuing. "I stood in a church and made a vow to her in front of God and witnesses."

"Yes, I know. I was actually there."

Evan's brows went up. "Daddy, you were the other man who left right after the ceremony?"

Gordon turned to face her. "Yes, Punkin' Pie, I was. And I

heard him say a lot of nice things to you. About being a part-ner and sharing adventures. I don't know if he meant any of it, or if that was just your cover. But you know what I didn't hear him say. I didn't hear him mention love." Gordon turned back to Hedge, leaning to within inches of his face. "I will not hand my daughter over to someone who doesn't love her."

Hedge exhaled. "I wouldn't ask you to. Mr. Tyler, I love Evan more than anything in this world. And I did mean every word I said in that chapel. Every word and then some." Hedge reached out for Evan's hand. "And not only that, but Evan loves me, too."

Gordon faced her, squinting. "Is that so, baby girl? Do you love him?"

Evan punched her dad in the shoulder. "You know I do."

"And you meant what you told him? When you stood in that church and committed your life to him, before God and everybody?" Gordon waited for her response.

"Yes, Daddy. I meant it."

Gordon nodded and offered his hand to Hedge. "Then all that's left is dotting the i's and crossing the t's."

"Oh my goodness gracious! Daddy, stop." Evan pressed her eyes closed and shook her head.

Hedge knit his brows together and shrugged. "Actually, we used our real names, and there is an official license registered. So technically, we are good."

Evan grabbed Hedge's arm. "That's not what he meant." She shook her head. "Which room is his?"

Hedge pointed to the door across the hall. "That one."

"Okay. You wait here. I'm going to assure him that you haven't *crossed my t* yet. I'll be right back." Evan patted Hedge's arm as he walked to the other side of the elevator door. Gordon was grinning like a contented cat as he opened the door to his room.

"That did the trick, eh?" He chuckled as he tossed his bag inside.

"I can't believe you did that. You're a mean man." Evan leaned against his shoulder for a second. She inhaled the smell of sweat and unsmoked cigars. "Get a shower. I'll holler in an hour."

"He loves you. I knew it at the wedding ceremony. Maybe before that. You know it, too. You just needed to hear him say it." He shrugged. "I got him to say it."

"I love you, Daddy." Evan squeezed herself into his bear-hug.

"Love you, too." He rolled his shoulders back and stretched. "Your momma's gonna want a reception at the community church for all her friends. Probably before Thanksgiving. And think pink."

"I know." She kissed his cheek. "Get some rest."

Evan turned back toward Hedge. There was so much to do, and so much to discuss that she didn't know where to begin. He took her hand as soon as she was in reach. Her stomach fluttered. He opened the door and scooped her into his arms, carrying her into their room.

"I don't have a house for us, so this will have to do for now."

Evan grabbed his neck and kissed him. She didn't stop for a breath as he lowered her feet back to the floor. She pushed him against the wall and leaned her whole body against his. She only broke the seal of their kiss when she opened her eyes and looked out to the balcony and saw the sun disappearing into the Caribbean Sea.

"Look at the view." She gasped and left him standing with his back to the door. She pushed open the sliding glass door and stepped out to the balcony, filling her lungs with the fragrant night air. The nearly full moon created white glitter over the black water. The beach below was aglow with tiki torches surrounding the revelers enjoying their vacations. Between the dark sea and the light sand, danced a ribbon of white foam, swaying in and out.

"It's just lovely." Evan sighed. "I'm going to enjoy every minute of it." She rocked her head back. What was *it*? The mission? Her career? Both in shambles. Their time in the Caribbean? Bound to be dangerous. Even her relationship with her dad had issues.

Her situation with Hedge? Yes, Evan would enjoy that. Married. It still hadn't sunk in. They'd only known each other for two months, but it had been immersive. She knew him better than men she'd dated for much longer. She was well past the everything-is-magical stage. *Shoot, he was downright infuriating most of the time.* But she loved him.

An ugly thought flashed through her brain. Did Hedge just say that he meant all those things to keep from fighting with her dad? No. But, what if he did? Fear started to creep up her spine. She had meant every word she'd said, and a lot more. She had been surprised by his vows, but she'd spent plenty of time thinking about how she felt for him. It felt sincere. It felt real.

"This is the first time I've been to the Caribbean," she whispered, hoping a break in the silence would ease her nerves. Hedge didn't respond. She realized suddenly that he wasn't standing behind her as she'd supposed. She turned around to see him still inside the room, on his phone. She smiled in his direction and took a seat on one of the lounge chairs. A few seconds later he tossed his phone onto the sofa and joined her outside.

"Who was that?" she asked. "News on Klim?"

Hedge shook his head and sat on the opposite chair, facing her. "No, actually that was your father. He says he's tired and that he's going to order up dinner and then go to bed early. He'll see us in the morning."

Evan nodded and drew a deep breath. "Yeah, a twenty-hour day really wears you out."

Hedge dropped from the chair to his knees in front of her. "I didn't ask you. I'm sorry I didn't ask you."

She wanted to reply with, *Ask me what?* But looking into his eyes, she knew. "I told you not to ask."

"I know, but I should have anyway." Hedge reached out and took her hands in his. "I want you to know that my word is my bond with you. But I also understand that I sprung it all on you without any warning. Using our true names, going through a real ceremony. So if you need some time, I get it. Take whatever you need. But when things get sorted out—when you're ready to talk—I do want to be your husband."

Evan's heart pounded against her ribs until she wondered if Hedge could hear it. She held tightly to his hands. She forced herself to breathe. In. Out. In. Out. "You're a good man." Her voice rattled with emotion.

"No, I'm not. I'm selfish. I want you. I need you. I'm just willing to wait for you."

She took a deep breath and smoothed her hair back from her face. "Do you want to know what I need?"

He leaned closer.

"I need a shower."

Hedge chuffed. "Of course." He leaned back on his heels. "Why don't you take a nice hot shower, and I'll order us something to eat. You'll feel better."

Evan took his hands and stood, tugging him up with her. Yes, she was certainly enjoying every minute of this. "You order dinner for us. That's a good idea. But I'm exhausted. I'm afraid I'm gonna need someone to wash my hair."

His face changed expression instantly. The corners of his lips widened a fraction of an inch both ways. "I'm your man."

"Yes, you are." Evan pressed her lips to his, reaching her fingers around his biceps. She pulled his arms around her. She leaned into his warmth, wishing they were on their honeymoon. She could use a week or two of this.

Evan pulled away from his embrace and ambled back inside. Before losing eye-contact, she shot Hedge her most seductive smile, though it was unnecessary. The electricity sparking between them nearly singed her skin.

She quickly undressed in the bedroom, leaving a trail of clothes to the bathroom door. She gasped at the luxurious egg tub in front of the glass wall overlooking yet another ocean view. Hedge had her toiletry bag open and ready on the marble vanity. She quickly used the toilet, started the shower warming, and then brushed her teeth.

Once in the glass front shower, she let the hot water run over her shoulders while she waited. Another minute later she heard his voice from the other side of the steamed glass door.

"Why do women always have to bathe in boiling water? How do you still have skin on your body?"

The door opened, and Hedge stepped inside with her. She let her gaze roam over his body. She had always blushed at the thought of Michelangelo's *David*. This was not that. His body was chiseled, but not from marble. Pure fire and flesh. *Oh, goodness gracious!* She slapped her hand over her mouth, unsure whether she'd said that aloud or not.

His expression was one of pure delight. His body responded to hers as he stepped closer. He held out his hand, and she pulled him against her.

Hedge grimaced when the water hit his skin. "Boiling," he repeated.

Evan tried to relax, but his skin felt hotter than the water. She smiled when she looked up into his eyes. She reached for the little bottle of shampoo. "You ever done this before?"

Hedge grinned, squinting as the water glanced off her body and into his eyes. "Not like this. No."

Evan took a half step back and squeezed some shampoo into his right palm. She started to turn her back to him, but he gently held her in place, facing him. He stretched his arms over her shoulders and rubbed his hands together over her head, working up a lather. He worked his fingers through her hair from root to tip, massaging the foam into her red silk tresses.

"Harder," she whispered, tightening her embrace around his back. She could feel the scars over his shoulder blades and ribs.

"Excuse me?" Hedge stepped back and looked her in the eye.

"You can scrub my scalp harder." She flashed her wicked-est smile. "If you don't scrub harder, this will take all night."

Hedge closed his eyes and dipped his chin. "And what's wrong with that?"

Evan grasped his hips in her hands and pulled him close again. "I have more to do tonight than just washing my hair."

His fingers massaged her scalp vigorously, and he turned her so that her hair was in the shower stream. He laughed as a dollop of lather splashed onto his shoulder. His hands followed the suds as they ran down her back and over her hips.

She enjoyed his touch as much as she loved finally touching him. She reached her arms around his neck and pulled his lips to hers. She felt her body flush with heat again. He slipped his hands around the back of her thighs and lifted her, turning her back against the warm tile wall. Evan's breathing quickened with her pulse, as their bodies became one.

Heat. Water. Steam. A few minutes of their voices echoing in the shower with rhythm and harmony, and the soles of her feet shot flames up her legs and through her lungs. The crease in Hedge's forehead deepened for a second. He closed his eyes and held her more tightly as the crease smoothed and he exhaled a moan into her ear.

She thought maybe she would die, but if so, this was definitely the way she wanted to go.

CHAPTER TWENTY-SEVEN

The aroma of dark roasted coffee tickled Evan's nose, coaxing her to wake. She let her eyes open to a squint. Enough to see that the sun was up, and so was Hedge. She sat up in bed and propped the pillows against the white enameled headboard that stretched to the ceiling. It had a floral pattern cut into it, and it was backlit, creating a nice glow behind her.

Hedge carried in a steaming cup of black magic and placed it on the nightstand beside her. "I didn't want to wake you, but your father will be here in thirty minutes. He just called."

Evan rolled her eyes. "What if today we didn't worry about catching bad guys and saving the world? What if we spent the day at the beach, like other honeymooners? We can catch the bad guys tomorrow."

Hedge laughed and nodded. "What if we catch the bad guys first thing this morning, and then we can spend the rest of the week on the beach?"

Evan sighed as she picked up her cup and sipped. "There'll just be another bad guy show up."

"You're probably right." Hedge disappeared into the closet for a second and reappeared holding two dresses. He held out the red one. Wrap-style, above-the-knee.

She shook her head. "More for evening wear. You know this."

"I know. I just wanted to watch you try it on."

Evan pointed to the navy midi with the square neck and elbow-length sleeves. "That one is business." She noticed he wore navy slacks. "Will we be too matchy?"

He shrugged. "I'll wear the light gray jacket. It'll be fine."

The phone on the nightstand started humming. Evan picked it up, reading the name on the screen. "It's my momma." She raised her eyebrows high. "Why does Kirk always make sure my momma has my number?"

"Answer it. I'll be in the living room."

"Hey, Momma," Evan said with a spark in her voice.

"Hey, baby. How are you doin'?" Her mother's tone was light.

"I'm good. How about you? Is something up?" Evan took another sip and stretched her legs before swinging her feet to the floor.

"Why would you ask me if something is up?"

Evan knit her brows together. Her mother suddenly sounded sharp. "It's just early. You usually call later in the day. That's all," Evan explained.

"Well, your daddy woke me up when he called. You had asked me to let you know when I'd heard from him, so I am. He called this morning. Said he was in the Caribbean. He had a quick stop to make there before comin' back home." Maggie Tyler's twang became heavier the more agitated she was, and at the moment, Evan could hear the twang reverberating in the air.

"Momma, are you okay?"

"He told me."

Evan's imagination jumped to a hundred different things her dad might have revealed to her momma. She sat straight up in bed. "Told you what?" She tried to keep her tone calm.

"That you got married."

Evan almost collapsed into her sigh of relief. Of all the scenarios playing in her mind, this one was perhaps the easiest to address. "Well, yeah. I was going to call you. It happened really fast, and I just got caught up in it all. But, Momma, Hedge is amazing. He's a really good man. You will like him."

"That's what Daddy said. I just wish I could have been there for you. Daddy said you looked beautiful. Like a princess. He texted me a picture." She paused for a minute, and Evan scrambled for something to say. "Does he protect you?" Maggie added.

What a weird thing to ask. "What do you mean?" Evan's mother had always championed her daughter to do whatever she liked. She had always told her that she didn't need a man to take care of her.

"I mean, on all these jobs y'all do. He's got your back. You trust him completely, right?" More twang.

Evan cocked her head to the side, still trying to decipher her mother's question. "I do trust him. He takes good care of me." Evan tried to sound like any blushing bride. "Momma, I'm sorry I didn't call or give you a heads-up. I didn't mean to make you mad."

She heard her mother sigh. "I'm not mad, baby-girl. But I'm not stupid, either. You don't have to keep pretending. I know you're a spy, like your daddy."

"What?"

"Oh, come on, for Heaven's sake. I've known for a year now. You can't make enough money to dash here and there all over the world with a fashion blog that's just a bunch of re-blogs from other websites. And you're always telling me about magazine articles, but they never get published. It's hard to brag on your kid when the Garden Club ladies ask for proof." Maggie's accent softened a little. "I asked your dad point-blank a year ago in March. He said that he thought you'd tell me in time. You don't have to protect me anymore. I'm just as tough as you two."

Evan smiled. A weight she didn't even know she'd been carrying flew from her shoulders. "I know you're tough, Momma. And I'm glad you know."

"So answer the question. Does he protect you?"

Evan laughed. "Yeah, he does. We protect each other." Hedge walked into the room again. "Mom, I gotta go. I'm still in bed and Daddy is coming to our room in just a few minutes. I need to get dressed."

"Okay, but you call me tonight. I'm fixin' to get out for groceries this morning, but I'll be home after that." She paused for a moment. "I love you, Evan, and I'm so proud of you. I always have been."

Evan swallowed hard. "I love you too, Momma. I'll call you tonight. Bye."

Hedge nodded. "She knows everything, right?"

"I guess she does."

"Mothers are smart creatures." He slid the tie that hung loosely around his shoulders back and forth to get the ends in the right position before beginning his half-Windsor. "I never even had to tell my mother. My first day home after being re-cruited, she just explained that if I was going to be in intelligence, I needed to be smart first, and clever second."

"And does she know about me yet?"

"Evan, I told her about you the day we met." Hedge flipped the wide end of the tie over the narrow. "Now go get dressed. I'll feel a lot more comfortable talking with your father if you're not naked in the next room."

She laughed as she flitted into the bathroom to prepare for the day. Teeth brushed. Make-up on. Hair curled. Dressed. Thigh holster in place. Shoes in hand.

She heard the door to their suite open and close, followed by the energetic tones of her dad's voice. She stared at herself in the mirror. Something was itching at her brain.

"Your father is here." Hedge moved to stand behind her. He nuzzled a kiss on the side of her neck and then looked up, making eye contact with her reflection. "Is everything okay?"

"I am the happiest I have ever been in my life." She meant it, but her voice sounded somber, even to her.

"So what's wrong?"

"It's as though I'm not supposed to be happy. Like I'm waiting for the other shoe to drop. All of this. I don't know what to do with it." Evan took a deep breath and let it go. She reached her left arm around to Hedge's back and pulled him closer. "Am I being ridiculous?"

"Not ridiculous. You're just trained to know all the bad things that can happen." He turned her around to face him. "But that's all the more reason to enjoy what we have now." He folded her into a long kiss. When their lips parted, he took a half step back. "Now come in here and see your father."

Still carrying her shoes in her hand, Evan followed Hedge into the small living room where her dad sat, cradling his own cup of coffee.

"Good morning, Daddy."

Gordon nodded and placed his cup on the table at his side. "'Mornin,' Punkin. You look pretty. Got a little glow to your face."

"Don't." She sat in the armchair by the glass doors. She slipped her shoes on. "Momma called this morning." She sighed. "Why didn't you tell me that she knew?"

"She wouldn't let me. It was a game for her. Wanted to see how long you'd keep it up." He reached into his jacket pocket and pulled out a mini bottle of whiskey and two cigars. He turned to face Hedge. "I got you a wedding gift. These are the essentials for being married to a redhead. These little things have kept Maggie and me together for thirty-two years now."

"Daddy, that's ugly." Evan smirked and smoothed her skirt.

Gordon chuckled and handed the bottle and cigars to Hedge. "The whiskey is for when you argue. The trick is, as soon as the disagreement starts, you take a shot. Then you tell her she's right and take another shot. You won't ever win a fight with her, so you might just as well enjoy it."

"And the cigars?" Hedge held them under his nose and sniffed slowly.

"These are to help keep you from the argument in the first place. Before you say anything you might regret, you stick one of these in your mouth and bite down as hard as you can. Don't light 'em. Besides that it shortens their lifespans considerably, that'll probably just start a different fight. I only had two on me, but that should get you through 'til the weekend, anyway."

Hedge started laughing and tipped his chin in Evan's direction. "I appreciate these, sir."

"Awh, now you don't have to call me *sir*. Maybe just *Gordon*."

The men laughed for a second as Evan made faces. It was time for work. "We need to get plans rolling, or we're gonna miss all the fun."

Gordon leaned forward in his seat. "You're right. Now I wanted to share my intel with you, and see if it all jives with your info."

Matching her dad's forward lean, Evan nodded and held out her hand. "That sounds great."

Hedge picked up the notepad from the desk by the entry and sat at the other end of the sofa, closest to Evan. "I'll make notes if we need them. Go ahead."

"My sources tell me that Klim is flying in this morning to oversee some transaction for Ves' Mir. I haven't got a twenty on the meet yet, but I figured you probably had that piece." Gordon leaned back and crossed his right ankle over his left knee. Evan knew that meant he was pleased with himself.

Hedge shot a glance at Evan, and she shrugged her shoulders a fraction of an inch. After a silent exchange of brow and lip shifts between them, Evan sent him a hint of a nod.

"Our lead was that Klim was already here. Arrived yesterday or the day before. And we know about the transaction, but not one hundred percent that Klim would be present for it. We have someone else in our sights, too." Hedge sniffed.

Evan flipped her palm toward her dad. "How sure are you of your intel, because we're solid with ours."

Gordon pressed his fingertips together. "Bogdan Klim, mid-fifties, dark hair, medium height, boarded a charter from Kyiv overnight. He should be here at any moment if he's not here already."

"Well, we're hunting Bogdan Klim, aka Costa Alenko, mid-thirties. He has light brown hair and medium build. The transaction we want to stop is scheduled for this morning." Evan neither crossed her legs nor sniffed. She was not confident that the bank meeting was the same transaction as her dad's.

"Okay." Gordon squinted and grabbed his right ankle. "Is it possible we're not chasing the same Bogdan Klim?"

"That's what I'm wondering." Evan rocked her head toward Hedge. "The descriptions of the man are all over the place. Honestly, I'm hoping this bank meeting will clear some things up."

Hedge pointed the pen in his hand toward Evan. "We don't even know for sure that Klim will be there. We're following another lead with the bank. Kir—someone, rather, told us that Nastya Alenko, Costa's sister, had an appointment to make a withdrawal and funds transfer with the Ves' Mir account."

"But Nastya Alenko is dead, right?" Gordon knit his brows low.

"Yep," Evan answered. "Real dead. But apparently, Nastya doesn't let death slow down her business. She made the appointment earlier this week."

"So who is keeping the appointment?"

This time Hedge responded. "We're pretty sure it's Xandra Yakovsky. They're similar physically, except for height, which can be remedied easily by adjusting heels."

Uncrossing his legs, Gordon turned to face his daughter. "She's dangerous. She tried to kill you."

"Daddy, everyone tries to kill me. You know that."

Hedge stood up. "She'll be armed. I'll be there, and I was hoping you would, too. We're not letting Xandra get close to her. The woman is delusional, but she's not as fierce as Evan."

"And not nearly as well-trained," Evan added.

Gordon nodded. "That's true. So what's the plan? We go to the bank just ahead of the appointment and scare Xandra into helping us catch Klim?"

Evan scoffed and stood next to Hedge. "Xandra's unscare-able. Not enough sense to be afraid. We'll get there ahead of her, but then we have to be prepared for a quick take-down. If it takes too long, it will be messy. I think three against one makes for good odds against her brand of psycho."

Gordon nodded. "And what if Klim crashes the party?"

Evan picked up her Springfield, checked the magazine, and chambered a round. "That's why we're going to be prepared."

CHAPTER TWENTY-EIGHT

Palm trees lined both sides of the road to the Queen's Bank of Cayman, and there was enough breeze to ruffle the leaves. Hedge studied the street and the traffic as if a clue might jump out at him between the cars.

He glanced sideways at Gordon in the passenger seat. There was something he wasn't saying. Evan trusted him. That should be enough. But somehow it wasn't. Not quite enough. Hedge looked back into Evan's eyes reflecting in the rearview mirror. She seemed as though she was forcing calm.

Her gaze shifted from side to side, and Hedge could see the tiny crease between her brows starting to deepen. Something had her worried, too.

The only one in the car who appeared confident was Gordon Tyler. He was nodding his head to an inaudible song, thrumming his fingers on the top ledge of the car door to the same rhythm.

No, something was off. Hedge checked the lane beside him and quickly moved over and then made an abrupt left turn.

"Are we being followed?" Gordon asked. "I didn't see anyone."

Evan shifted in her seat to look behind them.

"No, I don't think so." Hedge made another left and rolled into the rear parking lot of a convenience store. He parked beside a silver pickup with Marlin Marina company logos on either side. "I want to be sure, though."

Evan reached up and squeezed his shoulder. "Best to be sure. And we have plenty of time."

Gordon nodded but didn't seem to reposition himself to

watch for other vehicles making sudden moves.

Hedge turned in his seat to face Gordon. "What is this? Really. You obviously know more than what you're telling us."

Gordon looked surprised. He shook his head and turned on a pleading expression, gesturing toward Evan. "What? Evan, he doesn't trust me. Tell him."

"Tell him what, Daddy?" Evan shook her head. "Right now I'm not sure what's going on with you either. You shared a little information—and I do mean little. And you took what we gave you without question. Now you're along for the ride, probably humming *Hotel California* in your head."

"But," Gordon started.

"But nothing," Evan continued. "I may be your daughter, but I'm not a child. I can see that you're not transparent with us. You're playing too close to the vest."

Hedge nodded. "Look, this isn't personal. I don't want to cause conflict between you and Evan. But if this mission is going to be successful... ."

Evan interrupted. "A mission that has dragged out too long and cost too many lives, Daddy."

Gordon turned his palms up in surrender. "I haven't given you everything I know. But part of that is because I'm not one hundred percent on it. If I say something and I'm wrong, it could cost you much more than this mission."

Hedge exhaled, not realizing he was holding his breath. "I understand what you're saying. Maybe you're trying to protect us. Maybe you just want to keep Evan safe. I understand that part completely. But keeping pertinent information under wraps at this point won't protect us."

"Daddy, I'm a big girl. I can take care of myself."

"She can, sir. You trained her well." Hedge hoped to earn more of Gordon's trust. "You can tell us. We've already lost our jobs with InDIGO. We're not trying to finish this mission for the agency. We're just trying to keep the world from descending into financial ruin."

Evan's father turned back to face her more squarely. "The thing is, I'm called the Broker because I have made some deals between agencies. Between countries, Between businesses. I'm good at negotiations. You and I have been given different information about Klim. Who he is. I thought your intel was faulty. That someone was trying to distract you. But I think perhaps the opposite is true. I think I was being manipulated."

"But your sources led you here." Evan now had a hand on both men's shoulders. "So we both have some common information." She paused for a second, glancing at Hedge and then Gordon. "Are we being played again?"

Hedge listened and let the wheels crank in his mind. "Not in the same way as with Cooper." He studied Gordon's expression. "We're being baited, aren't we?"

"What do you mean?" Evan asked.

Gordon smirked. "He means that someone is giving us the information we're looking for. They know who we're hunting, and they're throwing out breadcrumbs to match."

Evan dropped her hands into her lap and leaned back in her seat. "You think it won't be Klim or Xandra at the bank?"

Gordon shrugged. "I think you're right about Xandra. I suppose Kirk gave you that. He's a good man. He probably gave you Klim's description, too, which makes me doubt my source."

"Actually," Evan said, "I've found both descriptions of Klim in my research."

Hedge watched a truck drive past them slowly. "We have to move." He put the car in reverse and got back to the main street. "I think Klim is only as real as Brandon Hedger or Eve Taylor. He's a useful persona, probably worn by at least two different men, maybe more."

"That makes sense," Gordon said. Now he was more watchful of the traffic around him. "I was withholding information. But for a good reason, and I now I think I know what's going on. I think I'm being lured out. Being hand-fed. I have a reputation for doing my job without question. I think someone is looking to tie up loose ends."

"And we're just dangling in the wind right in front of you?" Hedge knew Gordon would never hurt his own daughter, but he wasn't so sure about how Gordon felt about him.

Gordon shook his head. "I shot the guy in Amsterdam because he was there to kill you both. I'm not going to turn on you now. I'll do whatever it takes to protect my daughter."

"I know that. But maybe whoever is luring you out is using us as bait. And maybe they don't mind if we all get caught in the crossfire." Hedge tightened his grip on the wheel. "We're wasting our lead talking about this right now. I just need to know that you're with us on this job."

Gordon inhaled a deep breath and let it out slowly. "You're the point man, Hedge. You give the order, and I'll follow. No questions asked. No hesitation."

Evan released a sigh, and Hedge could see her expression shift from worry to satisfaction. She reached forward to her father's hand and dropped an earwig into his palm. "I'm Tango, Hedge is Papa. You're—wait, you can't be Tango, also. Maybe Golf for Gordon?"

"You know how I feel about Golf."

Hedge didn't hesitate. Call signs should be the least worry for this job. "Bravo for Broker."

Evan nodded. "Bravo is good. Get it in your ear now, and we can do a sound check."

Hedge pushed his earwig into position and looked out the side window. "Papa check," he whispered.

"Bravo check."

"Tango check."

Hedge made one more turn and pulled into a space at the side of the bank parking lot. Nothing conspicuous. Close enough for an expeditious getaway, but not the spot in front of the door. Hedge wished for another sound in his ear. *Kilo check* would give him that extra boost of confidence. Hedge knew that if Kirk were online right now, he wouldn't be able to acknowledge the fact. But he hoped.

Pulling out a small round piece of silver jewelry, Hedge held it up to show the others. "A little bit of insurance from a friend back home." He snapped the sterling clip over one of his jacket sleeve buttons. "It will block the metal detectors from seeing any weapons we're carrying. I only have one, so make sure you're in a five-foot radius of me when you go through. And any weapons need to be on your person. It won't do a thing for an x-ray."

Gordon pulled a similar device from his pocket and snapped it over his jacket button. "I have one, too." He grinned. "Same friend."

Hedge turned in his seat to face both Evan and Gordon. "Basics. Evan and I will go in as a couple opening a new account. We'll insist on seeing Carol Freemont. There should be plenty of time before her meeting with Xandra."

Evan nodded. "We hope it's Xandra."

"Yes." Hedge angled toward Evan a little more. He knew she might have a little apprehension about being face to face with the woman who tried to kill them all just a few weeks ago, but he wanted her to know that he had her back. "We can take her again, you know?"

"I know." Evan smiled and nodded.

"And once in Freemont's office, we'll plant a micro camera and another little gem." He pressed a dime-sized disk of black metal into Evan's palm. "This works with Bluetooth. Just stick it to the back or side of her computer, and it activates a keystroke capture program for our home team."

Gordon knit his brows together. "Hacking into bank records is serious—even for our mutual friend. If this Ves' Mir company isn't doing anything illegal, if they didn't acquire their assets through fraudulent means, there's nothing any government can do to freeze their accounts. My research indicates their primary source of cash flow is from mining operations around the world."

Hedge tilted his head back and shifted his jaw as he brought it back to level. "Yes, but when Evan threw out the name Ves' Mir, I did some digging into the previous mine owners and their companies. Cooper bought them out, one by one after each of their CEOs had visited Anton's parties and stepped out with Xandra or one of her girls. They were all blackmailed into selling."

"All of them?" Gordon asked.

"Not quite every one." Hedge checked his watch again. "There were also two suicides, fours suspicious auto accidents, and at least two very suspect heart attacks. And one CEO, Jane Timmons, of Kodiak Mines in Idaho, who has been missing for nearly two years." He gestured toward Gordon. "I'm sure you'll agree that those situations raise questions of legality?"

"Certainly." Gordon tilted his head to the side until Hedge heard a quiet crack from his neck. "And what do I do?"

Hedge scanned the lot once more. "Neither Costa nor Xandra should recognize you on sight. So if you will stay out here and watch the door, you can alert us if either of them shows up early."

"I can do that. So I'm stuck in the car?"

Evan leaned toward her father. "If all goes well, we'll join you back here in twenty minutes. We want Xandra to make her meeting and transfer funds. That's how we'll be able to find the money and track it."

"But if they show up early, and you two are still in your meeting?" Gordon started digging in his inside jacket pocket. "Do I follow them in?"

"Follow your gut on that." Hedge handed Gordon the car keys. "I trust you."

Gordon took the keys in his right hand and reached back for Evan's hand with his left, slipping a business card into hers. "You're opening an account. Use this account number to transfer funds into the new one. It's untraceable, and it's for you, anyway."

Evan looked at the card and flipped it over, reading a number on the back. "Are you sure?"

Gordon squeezed her hand. "Yeah, Ev. The PIN is EDT06/07."

"My initials and my birthday?"

Gordon pulled his hand back, and Hedge could see the muscles in Gordon's jaw flexing. "I told you. It's for you."

Hedge would have liked to give Evan a few minutes alone with her father, but it would have to wait. They had lost too much time already. "We gotta go. You can wait another twenty minutes for that hug, right?"

Evan and Gordon exchanged glances. "Yeah, twenty minutes," they said in unison.

Hedge swallowed hard. *Twenty minutes.*

CHAPTER TWENTY-NINE

Slipping her hand into the crook of Hedge's elbow, Evan walked confidently through the bank doors, through the metal-detector disguised as a decorative archway, and up to the reception counter. She smiled at the woman security guard standing just behind the clerk. Both women were average height and build, very tan, with solemn expressions.

Outwardly, Evan was calm and polished. Her training as a fashion model more than paid for itself. Inwardly, her stomach was turning cartwheels. She credited her daddy's presence for her nerves. *Just do the job.*

The clerk at the desk looked up. She was just as polished as Evan. Maybe a few years younger. She wore a black pantsuit with a black-checked silk blouse and a gold scarf tied at her neck. Her gold knot earrings were at least eighteen carats, and her lipstick was Chanel Incandescente, Evan guessed. The woman's red lipstick was an almost-perfect match to the curl of red that had wandered from Evan's top-knot.

The woman flashed a big fake smile. "May I be of service?"

Evan returned the smirk. "Yes. My husband and I would like to open an account. We just got married." Evan squeezed Hedge's arm, hoping the clerk would notice the size of his biceps beneath the sports coat. Hedge nodded toward the clerk, and then the guard. He kept his mouth zipped, this time becoming the eye-candy for the job.

Both the guard and the clerk looked Hedge over from head to toe. Without looking at each other, they both smiled.

Evan leaned a fraction of an inch closer to the clerk. Enough to notice the series of five security monitors nestled beneath the polished maple countertop. "I'd prefer to speak with

Carol Freemont. A friend of mine recommended her services."

The clerk, who now moved her scarf to reveal a name tag stamped Melissa, tapped on her keyboard. "Ms. Freemont has another appointment in thirty-five minutes. Would you mind working with Deiter?"

Frowning, Evan turned toward Hedge and huffed softly. "Honey, you said that there wouldn't be a problem."

Hedge shook his head. "Don't worry. I'll call the senator right back and tell him what's going on. I'm sure he can straighten this out with Carol in no time."

Without blinking, Melissa shook her head. "You're just opening a new account?"

"Yes, ma'am," Evan answered.

"Well, that shouldn't take too long. I can get you in to see Ms. Freemont. Give me one minute to let her know you're here."

Evan sighed, satisfied. "That'd be jus' lovely. We have everything ready. It shouldn't take but a second." She knew it was a risk to let her accent run free, but what would be more natural than a Texas millionaire opening an off-shore account?

Evan took advantage of the wait time to scan the bank. High vaulted ceilings, polished gray marble floors, lots of dark-stained birds-eye maple furniture and cabinetry. There was a back door with an alarm bar. That seemed to be the only visible exit besides the glass front doors. Two tellers sat behind a half-wall with a black marble countertop. Beyond the clerk's desk was an archway leading to a hall with offices on either side. The main lobby was smaller than Evan expected, and she assumed more business was conducted behind the office doors than in the lobby.

"Mr. and Mrs.?" Melissa asked upon her return. Another woman with dark hair and Sophia Loren eyes stood behind her.

"Parker," Evan answered. "Honey, this will be the first official thing with my new name on it. Isn't it exciting?"

The brunette stepped out and offered her hand to Hedge in a less-than-firm shake. "Mr. Parker," then to Evan, "Mrs. Parker. I'm Carol Freemont. Thank you for asking for me. May I ask who recommended my services?"

Evan tucked her chin and smiled. "I think we might have a mutual senator friend?" Evan wasn't prepared to name names, but it seemed she didn't have to. Carol made convenient assumptions and didn't press the matter further.

"And you two want to open a new account with us?" Carol led them down the hallway to the second door on the left. After opening the solid wood door, she gestured to the client chairs in front of the wood desk. "Please, take a seat."

Evan chose the farther chair, closest to the computer tower, which was positioned in the "L" of the corner desk. As Hedge was about to take his seat, he stumbled on the edge of the area rug, stopping his fall with one hand on the desktop and one hand on the wall just below a photograph of Carol and four official-looking men.

"Oh dear," Evan gasped. "Honey, you have to be more careful. You could've hurt yourself." She helped Hedge into his seat, only glancing for a split second at the omnidirectional micro camera he'd stuck to the picture frame.

"I apologize, Ms. Freemont," Hedge gushed, taking his chair. "I'm not as agile as I used to be." He waited for her to take her seat behind the desk. "I hope I didn't tip your frame. I hate when pictures are out of square."

Evan loved this. The mere suggestion that a frame isn't level is enough to keep most people distracted, if only for a few seconds. As Carol turned to examine her photo, Evan placed her handbag on the narrow desk space behind the tower, slipping the capture device on the underside of the tower, completely out of sight.

"They look like important people there alongside you. Anyone we might have heard of?" Hedge stood again and stepped closer to the picture.

"Local celebrities, mostly. The one on the far right, though, he was a close friend of my family. He had a cabinet position in France, but he passed away earlier this month."

"Oh yes, I heard about that. So very sorry for your loss." Hedge sat back down and turned to face Evan.

She didn't dare look at the photo. She had been there when Gerard Boulette had ended his own life with a bullet through his brain. She'd been just out of arm's reach. Unable to stop him. One more death. One more reason to stop this avalanche before it takes anyone else.

"We simply want to start our life together with a new account." Evan swallowed hard and pulled the business card from her purse. Here is the account number and the bank's routing number. The account is in my name, as well as my daddy's. It's a wedding present."

She handed the card to Carol, who placed it on the top of her keyboard and started typing. "Yes, and do you want the same type of account? Interest-bearing savings?"

"That would be fine, thank you. Is there a limit to how often you can access the funds?" Evan made sure to ask the usual questions. "In case of an emergency?"

"Yes, we do have limits, but our terms are quite generous." Carol leaned more toward Hedge as she emphasized *generous*. "Three times a month you can access without fees. And even the fees are nominal."

"Good." Hedge nodded.

Evan knew it was part of the game, but she didn't like Freemont's flirtation.

"And the PIN for the original account?" Freemont asked.

"It's right here, at the bottom of the card." Evan had penciled in the number. "And can you please tell me the current balance? I haven't checked that in a month or so."

"Yes, just one second." Freemont typed a little more, then paused. She nodded as she read her screen. "The amount we'll be transferring is $267,908.18. Does that sound right?"

Evan almost swallowed her tongue and prayed that she was able to maintain a straight face. "Yes. That's right, isn't it, dear?"

When she turned to Hedge, she smiled. For the first time since they met, he looked genuinely surprised. "It's a little more than I thought."

"But you forgot about the last quarter's interest, didn't you?" She patted his arm. "You always do that."

In another ten minutes, they had given Freemont every scrap of information she might need from them, and Carol handed them each a card with their new account information on it. She also handed Hedge her personal business card. "If you ever have any questions, please give me a call."

The couple stood and took turns shaking Freemont's hand. Evan thought she heard a crackle in her ear and she froze in place for a second more. Nothing.

Freemont gestured to the door. "Is there anything more you need? If not, I'll let you show yourself out. I have another appointment in a few minutes."

"That's fine. It was a pleasure meeting you, Ms. Freemont." Evan waited for a second as Hedge opened the office door for her.

"The pleasure was mine." Freemont nodded with a grin. "And best wishes on your marriage."

Evan listened for another crackle, hoping. When she heard nothing, she stepped out into the hallway, and suddenly she was nose-to-nose with Xandra Yakovsky.

CHAPTER THIRTY

Rowan Kirk checked his watch for the third time in a minute. It was still 10:14 in the morning. He had pulled his room-darkening shades to the sill and had only his bedside lamp on. The InDIGO offices had been shut down for the rest of the week, and he was relegated to his personal computer. Not a big deal, but it was like driving a station wagon instead of a sports car. His home computer had all the same gear, but the work computer had the speed, especially when connected to the InDIGO network.

His coffee was still steaming. His brain was ready. He'd been listening all morning to his team. Of course, they couldn't know this. Any acknowledgment could blow the whole operation, and this one needs to go off without a hitch.

He had already dented a few laws, but that could be fixed with the right results. Fischer had never complained too much about the letter of the law, and he always seemed to have the right connections to get the deals made.

Kirk brought up the security camera feed of the Queen's Bank of Cayman. Multiple camera angles tiled down the right-hand side of his screen. His team should be arriving any minute. Like most security cameras, the feed was black and white, with a blurred and skittery display. Why would a bank that conducted million-dollar transactions on a daily basis not pop for a better system?

On the upper left side of his monitor, was a frame labeled OMNI. It was black. Inactive for now. Below that was his work window. Also black, but ready for hacking, searching, or any other action required. Kirk sat in his vinyl desk chair straightening his peripherals, exercising his fingers, and waiting. He hated waiting.

The car pulled into view of the bottom camera feed. He could see Hedge and Gordon in the front, and Evan in the back seat. The men put in their earwigs and ran through the comms check. He wanted to offer a *Kilo check* but didn't dare.

He listened as they ran through the basic plan. He nodded silently, wishing he could reassure them all that he was standing by to grab whatever video and audio of Xandra Yakovsky impersonating Nastya Alenko they could snag. He was ready to pinch her account number and passcode. She wasn't going to get away with this. And he hoped Costa Alenko showed up, too. That would be the perfect topping to Xandra's just desserts.

Kirk rolled his aching shoulders back, ready to get to work. He could still feel where Xandra's bullets tore through his right trapezius. Nearly two months, and it still hurt. Physically and emotionally.

He focused on the bottom right screen. Hedge and Evan got out of the car, and Gordon shifted to the driver side. It was showtime.

He studied the screens as Evan and Hedge moved from one camera's sight to the next. He watched them enter the bank, go through the security arch, and then on to the reception desk in the lobby. He was proud of his little button-cover device, but he considered it almost primitive compared to the Little Black Dress. The button device could jam a signal for a ten-foot diameter, which could allow unwanted weapons to remain undetected, too. Less control than the cloaking feature of the dress. Not as secure as Kirk liked.

After a few moments of conversation with the clerk, Kirk watched his friends move down a hall and disappear into an office. It took Hedge mere seconds to plant the OMNI, and suddenly he had picture and sound in the top left quarter of his monitor.

At the bottom of that quadrant ran a ticker-style feed of Ms. Carol Freemont's typing. The program auto-saved at ten-second intervals. Fast enough to keep up with her, but not so fast as to cause a drag with any other programs. She was logging-in to her station.

Movement at the bottom right caught Kirk's attention. Gordon had moved from his place in the car to just inside the bank lobby. *Why?* Kirk reviewed the other angles. A woman at the teller desk. A man with a Panama hat and khakis going into the restroom. Another man standing at the edge of the parking lot camera's view. Too hard to make out anything about him with the sun flares in the lens.

Freemont was typing again. Entering a routing number for a bank. Account name. Evan's. Amount to be transferred. *Nice.*

More motion on the security feed. Gordon was still just inside the lobby door. It looked as though he was on his phone, but Kirk heard nothing through his receiver. A woman entered. Tall. Blonde. He'd recognize that walk anywhere. It was Xandra, and she was early. *Crap.*

Kirk inhaled and swallowed at the same time, unable to do more than gasp. She barely stopped at the clerk's desk. He watched her barrel down the hall toward Ms. Freemont's door. He had to warn Evan.

CHAPTER THIRTY-ONE

"...Xandra!" Evan heard Kirk's voice crackling in her ear.

A shot of adrenaline surged through Evan's system. Xandra looked exactly as she had the last time Evan saw her. Tall, slim, with long blonde hair flowing over her shoulders. Supermodel posture and supermodel clothes. Today Xandra wore a blood orange colored resort romper, which matched the furious fire in her eyes.

Evan expected her to charge. Instead, Xandra rushed back down the hall toward the lobby. "Xandra, stop!"

She didn't. Not until she was halfway across the open room, nearly crashing into another man. Evan and Hedge followed quickly behind her. They recognized the man about the same time Xandra did. Average height, green eyes, light brown hair. It was Costa Alenko.

Evan could hear Hedge whispering to the clerk and security guard. "Get everyone to safety and call the police. We're international law." From the corner of her eye, Evan saw Hedge flashing credentials, and the women hurried down the corridor. The two tellers ducked behind their desks. Evan hoped they had another way out of the room.

"What are you doing here, Xandra?" Costa asked her as she inched back from him.

Evan scanned the room. Her dad was standing in the short hall that led to the restrooms. Another man stood just inside the entry arch. She had to blink a couple times before she realized who it was. Max Fischer, director of InDIGO.

Her mind churned. Was Fischer there to help them, or, as her dad's suspicious squint indicated, take them into custody?

Xandra looked at the floor for a second, then cut her eyes toward Fischer. That seemed to give her courage because she straightened her posture and leaned slightly toward Costa. "I came here to protect my share."

Costa scoffed and shot a glance at Fischer. "You mean you came here to pretend to be my sister. You came to steal Nastya's share."

Shaking her head, Xandra appeared to lose some of her confidence. "It's not like that."

Evan took a step forward to catch Costa's attention. "I think she was planning to take much more than Nastya's share of the money." Evan moved into Xandra's peripheral view. "You were planning to take it all, weren't you, Xandra?"

"I just wanted some insurance. I don't want to become disposable." Her hands trembled enough that everyone else could see.

This time Fischer responded. "I didn't release you to come here. I told you that I would take care of you."

"Like you took care of Nastya and Cooper?"

Fischer clicked his tongue. "Their blood isn't on *my* hands."

Evan realized she didn't have her Springfield drawn, and she was exposed in the middle of the room. She glanced back over her shoulder to see Hedge staring at her with a mix of worry and admiration in his expression. She needed to get to cover so that she could arm herself properly.

"Humph," Costa grunted. "Cooper killed Nastya in cold blood, and I still don't know why. I took care of Cooper. I didn't need orders for that."

Evan started moving back toward Hedge when her dad stepped out from the hall. "Just make sure that your liabilities don't outweigh your usefulness, Alenko. You and Xandra both need to be careful about that."

Hedge shifted closer, too. "There are three names on that account: Nastya Alenko, Michael Cooper, and Bogdan Klim. Do you inherit your sister's part, Costa? Or are you Klim?"

Evan noticed both Costa and Fischer grinning.

"I am not disposable!" Costa blurted out. He pulled a large knife from his waistband.

"I wouldn't be so sure of that, Costa." Evan shifted so that she could see both Costa and Fischer equally. "Fischer isn't the type to leave loose ends dangling. That's why you set Xandra free, isn't it? She was supposed to make a beeline for Kyiv and take care of us."

"I still found you." Xandra sounded as though she were pleading her case.

"And you ran."

"The day isn't over yet." Xandra balled her fists and growled.

"Xandra, dear." Hedge's voice was calm. "Even if you make it through us, Fischer isn't going to let you walk out of here."

Xandra huffed. "I'm going to be the Empress of Russia. He wouldn't dare touch me."

Evan stifled a laugh. "He's lying to you. Imperial Russia is no more, thanks to your Bolshevik ancestors. He used you to organize Anton and the Muses for blackmail. Now that they're gone, he doesn't need you."

"You are the liar! You don't know anything." Xandra glared and said something in Russian, which Evan was sure was unflattering. "Maxim has power. He can make me Empress."

Costa laughed. "You think he would waste so much time with you after taking years to put me in line for the position of Deputy Prime Minister?"

"I'd wager that after today, Fischer won't care who is where in any government." Evan glared directly into Fischer's icy stare.

He didn't blink. "You think I'm done? That I'm not leaving this building?"

Evan held her ground. "Oh, you're walkin' out of here. In cuffs."

Hedge stepped between her and Fischer. "And whether the gold standard becomes a reality or not, you won't benefit from it."

Fisher scoffed. "Idiots. I have more power than any of you can fathom. Only a fraction of that stems from gold." His voice was sheer confidence, lined with fire. "My currency is fear. Fear drives production. Fear drives prices. Fear drives policies."

Evan hoped to keep him talking. "A well-placed bomb, a small-scale coup, a perfectly positioned suicide. These are your medium?" Her heart raced. She had known too well the fear that these acts stirred.

He pursed his lips and almost rolled his eyes. "It doesn't matter which way the cookie crumbles, as long as I am the one stacking the deck."

Kirk's voice crackled into a chuckle. "That man butchers every metaphor." Kirk paused as Evan suppressed a laugh. "I'm getting all of this, by the way. Local LEOs are aware of your presence and standing by. You just do your stuff."

Costa brandished his blade, apparently to keep himself relevant. "And I'm at Fischer's side, to make sure he succeeds."

Rolling his eyes, Hedge approached Costa carefully. "If you think Fischer needs you any more than her," he pointed toward Xanda, "you're as brainwashed as she is."

Fischer pulled a revolver from his jacket pocket and casually pointed it at Evan. "This is all getting a little boring to me."

Costa quickly moved his knife toward Fischer. "Wait! Is he right? You're just using all of us?"

"The trick is knowing when someone has served their purpose," Fischer said, shifting his pistol toward Costa and firing.

The bullet hit Costa in the upper arm, sending his blade skittering across the floor.

Everyone moved to take what little cover they could. Before Evan made it to the end of the clerk's desk, Xandra plowed into her side, knocking her to the cold marble floor. She had been in this position before.

Evan could hear her dad's voice yelling at Fischer. Costa was whining, and Hedge was giving instructions to the security guard. Chaos was all around her, but she had to focus on Xandra.

She pulled at Xandra's hair and arms, but the blonde was quick. She already had her hands tight on Evan's neck. He fingernails dug in the back, and her thumbs pressed firmly at her windpipe. She pulled on a handful of hair and pushed her legs to the side to leverage her body out from under Xandra.

They were on their sides, and Evan wedged her right arm between Xandra's, prying her grip from her throat. Evan made a fist and punched Xandra's jaw. Not enough momentum to knock Xandra entirely away. They continued to struggle.

Evan could hear more gunshots. More yelling. *A little help would be nice.* But none came. She kicked and punched. Xandra returned every blow.

More shots. Costa fell to the floor with at least two shots to his head. Dead. From the corner of her eye, Evan could see her dad clutching his shoulder, blood on his sleeve. She pushed Xandra back for a second, long enough to see Hedge getting shot in the hand, his Walther flying away. Too much.

She tightened her fist again and punched Xandra squarely in her left collarbone. It snapped, just as clearly and loudly as it had two months before. Xandra howled and collapsed.

Evan stood before she realized she was still not adequately armed. Now Fischer held two pistols out, aimed. But neither was pointed at her.

"You choose, Tyler. Do I kill your father or your partner? Which shall it be?"

Gordon shook his head. "Don't think twice. You always choose your Papa."

Evan knew what he was telling her. He was sacrificing himself. She took a step toward Hedge.

"No, Evan. Save your father. Then save yourself." Hedge nodded and forced a smile through his pain.

There was no choosing. Evan could hear nothing more than her heart pounding in her ears. She looked at both the men she loved, one on either side of her.

"Sweet like sugar," Fischer said. "The consensus then is that I save you?" He pointed his pistol steadily at Gordon. "Too bad."

But as Fischer fired, another shot sounded, too.

The bullet meant for Gordon hit the wall behind him. The other shot tore through Fischer's knee, sending him to the floor, clutching his leg.

The security guard stepped forward, keeping her pistol trained on Fischer's head.

Gordon grabbed both of Fischer's weapons and pushed them away with his left arm. "You only cared about climbing the ladder, Max. You didn't have to do it this way. You were a good agent once. You were a good man."

Hedge looked back to the guard. "Are you alright?"

"Yes, sir."

"You did well." Evan nodded her direction. "May I borrow

your cuffs?"

The woman pulled her handcuffs from her belt and tossed them to Evan. She lowered her pistol and faced Hedge. "We have a med kit behind the desk. For your hand."

Evan smiled at Hedge, and he smiled back, knowing he would be fine. She patted Fischer down and cuffed his hands behind his back.

"I'm going to bleed out," he whimpered. "I need help."

Looking over his leg wound, Evan shook her head at Fischer. "That's not so bad. Trust me, I've seen worse."

Gordon stood and hobbled his way to the desk where gauze and tape and bandages were being organized.

"You okay, Daddy?"

"I'll be right as rain, Punkin' Pie. You take care of Hedge."

Evan smiled and winked at Hedge. "He's fine. I need to get Xandra fixed up." She grabbed a bandage wrap from the desktop and knelt beside the blonde. "I'll get your arm immobilized. And lucky you, you already know how long this takes to heal."

Xandra spat out a long stream of Russian curses as Evan wrapped her arm tight to her body.

"Well, that's not very lady-like." Evan cinched the last tail of the bandage around Xandra's tiny waist.

"You know Maxim is Klim." Xandra grimaced.

"We know." Evan put her hand to her throat, feeling the scratches. Her voice was hoarse.

"And you are just letting him go? He will do it again." Xandra yanked her free arm back to point at Fischer. "He will kill us all."

"He's not killing anyone else." Evan sighed. Even her breath scratched in her throat. "We're going to take him in."

Xandra scowled at her. "You are all stupid." She lunged

forward, knocking Evan on her butt. Xandra reached beneath the hem of Evan's skirt and grabbed the pistol before Evan could stop her. "I am taking him out!" she screamed.

Xandra fired two shots before Evan tackled her again, knocking her Springfield from her hand.

The first bullet went through Fischer's jacket sleeve, missing flesh. The second, however, hit him in the center of his chest. He looked as though he would say something, but almost instantly the color drained from his face. He slumped forward, dead.

"What happened?" Kirk's voice was as loud as the receiver allowed.

"Xandra. She just," Evan gasped. She was out of breath, scrambling to get Xandra under control. Evan had had enough. She brought her left elbow down on Xandra's right clavicle, and it snapped, too. Another yowl and Xandra was rolling on the floor, kicking her legs in protest.

"What did Xandra do?" Kirk asked in a frantic tone.

"She… killed… Fischer," Evan managed to say between gasps.

Kirk's voice shifted to a more official attitude. "I need a sit-rep."

"Can you get that from Hedge, please? My throat is sore from being strangled again." Evan looked back at Hedge and her dad, both of whom were being fawned over by Melissa and the guard. She staggered back to the desk, picking up her pistol on the way. "And Kirk, we need to talk about getting me a wardrobe with better access to my thigh holster."

Evan reached past the bandages and grabbed a roll of duct tape. She proceeded to wrap Xandra's arms to her body, ignoring her cries of pain and Russian swears. She listened to Hedge and her dad explain to Kirk what had happened and assisted the local officers as they managed the scene.

The medics arrived and checked everyone over. Evan, Hedge, Gordon, and Xandra all took a quick ride to the hospital. Costa and Fischer went to the morgue.

"Evan," Kirk's voice whispered after she was cleared for release. "You don't need to talk. I just want you to know. Xandra will be moved this evening to a secure location, as will the bodies of Fischer and Alenko."

"Good." Evan sipped on a cup of hot tea, waiting for Hedge to join her in the hospital corridor. "Do you have any leads for us to run down? Any loose ends to tie up?" Her throat still hurt, but the warm liquid helped.

"I'm taking care of all of that. It looks like Fischer was the top of the food chain. I've cracked his computers, both office and home. I'll wait for his phone and anything else he had on his person, but it looks like he spent this last week cleaning house. At least seven other agents have turned up dead. InDIGO is down to a skeleton crew." Kirk paused for a minute. His voice softened. "Evan, I'm glad you and Hedge are okay."

"Me, too, Red."

"I'll send you instructions in a few days. You all need some rest."

Evan set her cup on the tray beside the door as her dad was wheeled into the hallway. She looked at the nurse. "How long will he be staying?"

The petite woman smiled broadly. "Doc says just a day or two. He's lucky. He'll make a full recovery."

"Daddy, do you want me to stay up here with you?" Evan walked beside his wheelchair. "And I'll call Momma. Don't worry about anything."

Gordon laughed. "Don't you dare. I already called her and told her it was nothing. Don't you get me into more trouble." He waved his hand at her. "Now get back to your husband. Take care of him. You both can come to see me tomorrow. I'm gonna sweet-talk this nurse into letting me go home early."

Evan smiled as she watched her dad ride into the elevator with the nurse. Hedge joined her in the hall, his right arm in a sling, his hand wrapped in clean gauze.

"That man can take care of himself," he said. His left arm snugged her waist.

"I guess so," she sighed. "Kirk says we have to rest up here and then he'll send instructions. What does the doctor say about your hand?"

Hedge laughed and turned her to face him. He brushed his left hand over her shoulder. "I'm fine. No permanent damage. Let's go back to the resort."

Evan leaned close, careful not to crush his arm. "Are you gonna tell me about all the stuff I missed while I was wrestlin' with Xandra?" She could hear his heart beating through his shirt.

"Let's enjoy a few days of honeymoon first. We can deal with the White Witch later, okay?" Hedge gestured to the doors leading out to the parking lot. "Kirk sent a car for us."

"What about your hand?" Evan followed him out to the car. "You can't drive."

A black limousine idled in the driveway in front of them. "I don't have to, and neither do you." He opened the limo door for her with his left hand and slightly raised his slinged right arm. "As far as my hand goes, for the next week or so, you'll have to wash my hair."

CHAPTER THIRTY-TWO

"How are you feeling? Do you need another pain pill?" Evan asked Hedge as she brought their room service dinner of steak and lobster out to the balcony where he rested.

"No. I'm good." Hedge sat up from the reclining position. "Better than good. What about you? How does your throat feel?"

"Better." Evan's voice felt stronger. "Should I feed you, or can you eat left-handed?" She positioned the dinner tray on the low table between the lounge chairs.

"I can manage with my left if you'll cut up my steak first." Hedge smiled. "I'm still capable of almost everything, with a little help."

Evan shot him a wicked glance. "I know." She started slicing his dinner into bite-sized pieces. "Was it tougher for you this morning? Since we're married, I mean?" She studied his face for a reaction.

"Are you asking if I was more worried for you? No. You are the most capable woman I have ever known. Being married to you didn't change that." Hedge took a quick bite. "Was it tougher for you? After all, you had both me and your father to worry over."

Evan pondered the same thought she'd been rolling through her mind all afternoon. She hadn't been more worried. Not more than usual. It was as though nothing had changed. "It wasn't tougher. I thought it would be. I thought it was supposed to be. But even when Fischer told me to choose between you two... I wasn't worried."

Hedge nodded. "What were you thinking when he said that?"

After taking a slow sip of her pineapple juice, Evan sighed. "I was actually just looking for something to shoot him with. I know it's awful, and that he might have been more help to us alive, but when Xandra killed him, all I could think was that he got better than he deserved."

"Remind me not to cross you."

"Every single day." Evan took a bite of her butter-drenched lobster. "My momma is anxious to meet you." For the first time in a long time, Evan felt homesick.

"Is she a tall red-head like you?" Hedge ate a few more bites of his dinner.

Evan drew a deep breath and released it. "She's a short red-head. I get my height from my daddy and my fire from my momma." She looked out at sea for a minute, letting the breeze push her hair away from her face. "What about your family? When can I meet them?"

"Now don't do this."

"Do what? You already know my dad. I want to meet your folks, too."

Hedge shrugged. "It was going to be a surprise. Your father is going to be upset at me. We have it worked out for both our families to meet next month. Your mother is already planning the reception." He shook his head. "What am I supposed to tell your father?"

"Tell him I'm especially gifted in extracting secrets." She shifted around the table to sit beside him. "I am really good at that, right?"

"I will not be telling him any such thing."

Evan leaned over Hedge and placed a line of kisses across his jaw as she unbuttoned his shirt and peeled it back from his shoulder. She trailed her lips gently down his neck and across the top of his chest.

"Your dinner is getting cold," Hedge said, though he shifted back in his seat making her task easier.

"Don't care." Between kisses.

"Me neither," he said, wrapping his good arm around her body.

A knock at the door. They both froze in place.

"It's me," came the sound of Gordon through the door.

Evan sat up and hurried to the door, opening it and pulling her daddy inside. "How'd you get out of the hospital so quick?" She directed him to the couch.

"Bella, that's my nurse, she talked to the doctor for me. She assured him that I would have perfect care from my daughter and son-in-law. So I checked myself out and headed over. I went back to my old room, but the key didn't work."

"Yeah, we checked you out. You were supposed to be in the hospital for two more days." Evan looked out to the balcony where Hedge was getting up from his chair. "Just sit here, and I'll bring in our dinner. There's plenty for you."

Gordon sat at the end of the cream leather sofa. "Something light, I hope."

"Surf and turf," Hedge said as he came back through the sliding glass doors.

"Perfect." Gordon eyed the plate as Evan began slicing her own steak into bite-sized chunks for her dad.

Evan sat back in the armchair facing the men as they began poking at the cubes of food on their plates. "You two are a pair. Mirror image."

Gordon glanced down at the sling on his left arm and pointed his fork at Hedge. "At least I had the sense to get shot on the left side, and not my right."

Evan glared at her dad. "You do know that's the side your

heart is on?"

"But I never take my heart with me when I'm on a job." Gordon took a bite and looked at Evan's glass of juice.

She shook her head and brought him a glass of water. "You can pretend to be as tough as you like. But you had your heart with you today."

He smiled and nodded. "Yes, I did." He took another bite and nodded toward Evan. "Are you going to eat anything?"

Evan laughed. "I'm done for now. I'll call down and see if we can find you another room."

"If not, I can stay here. I'll sleep on the couch."

"No, no." Evan shot a hot glance at Hedge. "I'll find a room for you. We're still enjoying our honeymoon, remember?"

"Oh, yeah." He laughed. "You don't need to worry over me, Evan. I'll find my own room. Look at this poor guy." He waved his fork at Hedge again. "He needs your help. Get over here and take care of him. Your old man can see to himself."

Hedge nodded and shifted in his seat to make room for Evan beside him.

Gordon took another bite and then stood, stretching as far as his sling allowed. He lumbered to the hotel phone and made a quick call. "Yes, please. This is Gordon Tyler. I was previously in room 322. Checked out earlier, but it seems I'll be extending my stay. Could you find another suite for me and send the key up to 319, please?" He paused and nodded. "Thank you kindly." He cradled the receiver. "No problem at all."

Evan laughed. "Then come sit and eat a little more while you wait."

He had barely got another bite into his mouth when there was another knock at the door. "Evan, can you get that?"

Evan sighed and stood. For a split-second, she thought she saw Hedge exchange a side glance with her dad.

When she opened the door, she saw her momma standing in front of her. She saw only a flash of a bright smile before being engulfed in a tight hug. Evan's body still ached from her fight, but as soon as she was in her momma's arms, the pain melted away.

"Surprise!" Maggie whooped. "Are you surprised?"

"Yes, Momma, I'm surprised." Evan led her mom into the little sitting room with the men. "Whose idea was this?"

"Mine," both Hedge and Gordon said at the same time.

"Actually, it was my idea," Maggie said. "You all get to go gallivantin' all over the world while I'm back home holdin' down the fort. I figured if we were celebrating a new addition to the family, I should be there. Here, rather." She smiled broadly. "You guys are on your honeymoon. We can be on our second honeymoon."

Hedge stood and offered Maggie his left hand. "It's a pleasure to meet you, Mrs. Tyler."

Evan watched her mom take stock in Hedge, working from the deck shoes up. "I'd say the pleasure's all mine, but that privilege belongs to my daughter. Evan, honey, you done good."

Evan blushed and shifted the conversation quickly. "What room are you in? I suppose you were the call Daddy made a few minutes ago?"

"Yes, and I was able to get the room he had this morning." Maggie gestured to Gordon. "I don't mean to be rude, but I haven't seen my husband in three weeks. We'll see you two in the morning. Late morning." She paused as Gordon followed her to the door.

Evan kissed her dad's cheek and then turned to her mother. "The doctor said he didn't hurt anything vital. It was a through-and-through. He still needs to get some rest while the muscles heal."

Maggie looked at Gordon and sighed. "I've seen worse." She waved back at Hedge. "We'll see you at lunch."

Evan closed the door after them, and when she turned back to the room, Hedge was standing right in front of her. "Wow. Here you are."

"Here we both are." He lowered his lips to hers. "I like your parents," he murmured through the kiss.

"That was the surprise. Not the thing in another month, right?" Evan pulled his body against her.

"Oh, we can arrange for a big family thing whenever you like." He kissed her again. "I know how good you are at extracting secrets, but I'm really good at keeping secrets, too."

"Are you keeping anything else from me, husband?" She again worked her way through his shirt buttons.

"That's for you to find out, wife."

"You don't mind if I use whatever means I deem necessary?" Evan whispered in his ear.

"I'm counting on it."

CHAPTER THIRTY-THREE

Evan and Hedge waited under the black awnings of the Pub St. Michel. A warm, late summer rain had just begun, so they stepped just inside the heavy double doors of the Parisian establishment.

"Table pour deux?" It was the host with the Poirot mustache.

"Non, monsieur," Evan flashed her smile. "May we please wait at the bar for our friend?" She shifted into her Texas drawl, and Mustache seemed to remember her.

"Oui," he said gesturing to the stairs at his right. "Monter."

Hedge followed Evan up to the bar. They were a little early for their meeting, but not too early. Sitting on the middle barstool, smiling broadly, was Kirk. He hopped down at once.

Evan hurried into his outstretched arms. "Red, you're already here."

"Of course. Last one to arrive picks up the tab, right?" Kirk stepped back and shook Hedge's hand vigorously. "All healed, brother?"

"Healed up fine. Your girl here has been taking good care of me." Hedge held Evan's hand as she claimed the stool between the men.

"My girl?" Kirk said, shaking his head. "No, sir. This one is all yours."

Hedge ordered each of them a drink, and the barman went right to work.

Tilting her head toward her old partner, Evan took a more serious tone. "Red, why didn't you ever explain to me about your poker buddies? And why didn't you tell me that my daddy was one of them?"

Kirk exchanged a grimace with Hedge and then fixed a conciliatory expression on his face. "Sure. You're in the middle of a runway show in Milan, and I say, 'Oh, by the way, I've known your dad for years. Turns out he and I are on the same super-secret elite forces team. In our spare time, we hunt down people and stuff that doesn't *officially* exist and put them to use to save the world.' How would that have gone over with you?"

She gave a little huff. "Well, you could have said *something*."

"You're always packing heat, and I didn't want to upset you. I have no delusions—you could take me out in a hot second." Kirk laughed. "Besides, we do get together for a poker game once a month."

Hedge stifled a chuckle as he tipped his drink toward Kirk. "Wise man."

Evan rolled her eyes at both men. "Both of you are ridiculous. Trying to protect me. Don't want me to worry about my daddy."

Kirk nodded. "You're welcome."

The three friends laughed and talked and sipped for almost an hour until the rain tapered to only the slightest drizzle.

"Are you ready to go?" Kirk asked. He glanced at his watch.

Evan felt a fluttering of butterflies dancing in her stomach. Hedge was smiling almost as broadly as she was. "Yes, let's go."

The threesome hurried over puddles and through traffic to the quaint storefront butcher's shop a few blocks from the pub. The brass bell clanged as they went inside.

Kirk saluted the man behind the counter and led them all through a small arch and up the stairs. At the head of the stairway was another archway, framing an old oak door with obscure glass in the top.

Kirk tapped on the glass.

"Come."

Kirk held the door open for his friends. Evan had never seen the room before, but it was just as she expected. An authentic Degas hung over the credenza behind the massive oak desk in front of them. To one side, a large armoire stood open.

After only a second, Eleanor McKinnon-Grey stepped from behind the armoire door, holding out a garment bag.

Evan's heart pounded. She blinked away a wave of lightheadedness when she realized she'd been holding her breath.

"It's wonderful to see you, Elle." Evan laughed. "May I still call you Elle, or should I call you *Director*?"

"Elle—always." She hung the garment bag on the outside of the wardrobe. "And it's great to see you, too. All of you." She gestured to the chairs on their side of the desk. "Gentlemen, you can have a seat. Evan, come over here and meet your new best friend."

Evan rounded the end of the desk to stand in front of the black bag.

Elle started to pull down the zipper and paused. "I should let you do the honors."

"I can't." Evan held out her hand to show Elle. Her perfectly manicured fingers trembled. "I feel like I'm going on my first date. You'll have to unzip it."

"Of course." Elle pulled the zipper to the bottom of the bag. She removed a pair of black heels and set them carefully on the desk. Next, she revealed a slim, open box containing the body-armor corset. "And last, but not least," Elle said with a flourish, "the improved Little Black Dress."

Evan took the hanger and dress from Elle as soon as it was

free of the bag. The fabric was softer than she remembered. Like the prototype, it glowed like a black pearl. But this beta version had slightly different details.

It retained the straight strapless neckline as well as the side ruching that allowed Evan to adjust the skirt length, but the new LBD included a wrap-style skirt. Evan inspected the hemline closely. The extra drape of fabric concealed a high side slit, making access to her thigh holster much more convenient and efficient. That difference alone warmed her heart. She perused the corset for the notch-switch that manually activated the SEM pulse. Same as before, at the center of the neckline. Returning to the dress, she searched for the waistline buttons that powered the dress up or down. Missing.

"You don't need the buttons anymore." Elle gestured to Kirk.

Kirk leaned back in his chair and crossed his arms over his chest. "This dress is undetectable to electronic sweeps. It emits a smaller power signal than a typical key fob. You'll never need to go into blackout mode."

It was perfect. Evan held it to her body, savoring the silk against her skin. She felt a moan of delight rise from her gut. She wasn't sure whether she had made an actual noise or not.

Seeing the silly grin on Hedge's face, she decided she had, and blushed for good measure.

"Are you ready for the first field test?" Elle asked.

Shifting her gaze from Hedge to Kirk and back to Elle, Evan nodded. "I'm ready for anything."

THE END